STORE

Love in STORE

HOLLOW CREEK, BOOK 2

PENNY ZELLER

Dedicated to Nanie, who went to be with Jesus during the writing of this book. Thank you for being the best grandma a girl could have. I miss you so much, but will see you again.

God is our refuge and strength, a very present help in trouble.
Therefore will not we fear, though the earth be removed,
and though the mountains be carried into the midst of the sea;
Though the waters thereof roar and be troubled,
though the mountains shake with the swelling thereof.

~ Psalm 46:1-3

CHAPTER ONE

HOLLOW CREEK, MONTANA, 1912

THE PAST EVENTS, NONE of which were her doing, had come to this.

McKenna Chapman peered at the passing landscape through the Model T's window. The Bitterroot Mountains, still capped with snow, stood strong against the meadows and prairies. Antelope foraged in the fields for something to eat, and in the distance, cattle dotted the countryside.

Until last year, McKenna hadn't paid much notice to the mountains, the ranches, antelope, or anything outside of Missoula. But now, as a passenger in an automobile driven at a pace slower than the movement of a three-toed sloth, she not only viewed her surroundings, but she viewed them for an eternity. At a pace Father's driver would never have dared to drive.

Not that she could fault Morris, the precious elderly man behind the wheel. Nor his wife, Vera, who sat beside him. After all, Aunt Julia Mathilda's friend, Emilie Evanson, could have easily not offered her hired help to transport McKenna the two hours from Missoula to Hollow Creek, a town she'd never heard of. Instead, McKenna could be at the mercy of some other service since the train had yet to complete the spur to the town.

McKenna worried her lip. What if she didn't succeed at this opportunity to manage Aunt Julia Mathilda's new boutique? How would she assist Mother and Father, and more importantly,

1

Arrosa? She stared down at her hands—her red and scaly hands with fingers still chapped from assisting Mother at the laundry. The irony wasn't wasted on her—instead of having their laundry washed by the help or taking it to a laundress, now Mother and McKenna washed the laundry for others.

Morris, with enormous eyes magnified behind his spectacles, took his gaze from the road and stared at Vera for a bit too long, all the while driving.

Vera tittered. "I do love you, Morris."

"And I you, Vera."

It was then McKenna realized they were driving on the wrong side of the road. Did Morris not realize his inattention?

An automobile speeding in the opposite direction approached. The driver honked his horn, startling Morris, who swung the wheel and righted the vehicle just in time to avoid a collision.

"Oh, dear!" Vera held a hand to her bosom. "McKenna, are you all right?"

"Yes, ma'am."

"Forget sometimes that the road is a narrow one," Morris said.

Vera nodded, her oversized hat sliding to one side. "Automobile drivers these days! Thank the Good Lord above that other driver had the sense to miss us." She paused. "Shall we sing to relax our nerves?"

"Indeed."

The couple's voices rose over the engine's roar and the sound of the wind. In near-perfect harmony, Vera's alto voice combined with Morris's rich baritone, and they sang:

My Bonnie lies over the ocean,
My Bonnie lies over the sea,

My Bonnie lies over the ocean,
Oh, bring back my Bonnie to me.

McKenna remembered visiting the ocean with her family three years ago. They'd traveled to California and spent a day on the coast. Back then, McKenna hadn't appreciated the ocean's beauty or the time with her family. She hadn't cared about the seagulls or the stunning blue water.

Several years ago on a ship to London, she'd been bored and unaffected by the dolphins who played in the ocean when she'd ventured out on deck. She and Arrosa instead grumbled that they had to be confined on a ship when they'd much rather be shopping at fine boutiques in New York City.

Regret, despondency, and discouragement settled in her mind.

Vera and Morris paused for a moment, and Vera glanced back at her. "How are you, dear?"

"I'm afraid I'm not good company today."

Morris shifted in his seat. "Did she say she'd like to accompany us with our singing?"

"Fantastic!" Vera clapped her hands.

But McKenna wouldn't be accompanying them in their singing. Instead, she would be dwelling on the fact that she must—absolutely must—succeed at this endeavor. Arrosa's life depended on it.

With Morris's help, McKenna managed to hoist her small trunk up the stairs and into the apartment above the new Miss Julia Mathilda's Fine Dresses. Tomorrow she would commence unpacking her own things as well as organizing all of the merchandise previously delivered and awaiting her downstairs.

A twinge of excitement rippled through her. While this was not her first choice for the road her life had now taken, she would make the best of it. And truth be told, working in a boutique was far better than laundering, although she would do whatever was necessary to support her family.

This paid better, which meant more desperately needed funds for Mother and Arrosa.

McKenna bid Morris goodbye, assured Vera she'd be fine settling in on her own, and peered about the dreary apartment. Peeling yellow wallpaper barely clung to the walls, the floor was coming up in spots, and a water ring marred the center of the ceiling. A table with two chairs, a dry sink, shelves, an icebox, and a pot-bellied stove were the only larger items in the main room. Pots, pans, and an assortment of mismatched plates and cups cluttered the shelves. At least those were things she wouldn't have to buy. Dulled curtains hung on the dirty windows, and she peeked out to the main street and boardwalk below. Passersby, an occasional automobile, and plentiful horses and wagons went about their business below.

In the only other area of the apartment—a tiny bedroom the size of the washroom in her old home—a shabby bed with a thin mattress, flat pillow, and faded quilt stood in the corner. She would utilize her trunk as both a nightstand and to hold her meager belongings.

Homesickness flooded her, and a single tear surmounted the bridge of her nose. So, so unlike her former bedroom at her parents' mansion with its comfortable bed, pink quilt, paisley wallpaper, chaise lounge sofa, colorful rug, and inviting fireplace.

Things would never be the same again, that much she knew.

But she'd not surrender to the most recent events that had befallen her family. She took a deep breath and removed her hat. Aunt Julia Mathilda gave strict instructions on how to manage the shop, and if McKenna was to succeed, she'd have to work hard. After all, it was doubtful her aunt would be amenable to paying her wages if she failed to be successful in selling copious amounts of wares.

Shouldn't be too difficult in a city like Missoula, but in a village like Hollow Creek? Doubt threatened and she drew a breath and held it before finally releasing it. McKenna would visit the mercantile for some necessary provisions, return home and unpack some of her belongings, then retreat to the boutique. She couldn't wait for the latter.

It was nearly nine o'clock when McKenna finished all of the duties that beckoned her in the apartment. Where had the day gone? It didn't help that she'd arrived in Hollow Creek at 4:30. That hadn't left her much time to pay a visit to the mercantile before it closed, prepare a humble supper, and do her best to organize the apartment.

If Arrosa was here, oh, what fun they'd have! It wouldn't matter that the living quarters left much to be desired. They would do as they had so long ago as young girls and pretend to be on an adventure. Reality reminded McKenna that, at twenty-four, she was now a mature woman instead of a young girl. A spinster who must do her best to ensure Mother and Arrosa had food to eat and Arrosa the medical care she needed.

McKenna washed the few dishes she'd dirtied and organized the existing plates and cups on the shelf. Perhaps she could venture downstairs and begin organizing the items for the shop.

She wouldn't be sleeping tonight anyway, what with her fraught nerves, so why not go there now? The town appeared safe enough.

The sun had begun to set and the temperature was cooling, so McKenna put her wrap around her shoulders, and lantern in hand, descended the stairs, marched through the alleyway, and rounded the corner to the boutique. Few folks were out this time of night, and it was still light enough for her to see fairly well. She could only imagine how exciting it would be to decorate the boutique however she saw fit. To hang the clothes, dress the mannequins, and arrange the jewelry. To add her own personal flair to it.

To make Mother and Father proud.

McKenna unlocked the door and closed it behind her. Aunt Julia Mathilda mentioned she hired a freighter to deliver the wares as the spur to Hollow Creek wasn't yet complete. McKenna scanned the nearly vacant room. Did the shop have electricity? That would be something for her to investigate tomorrow. For now, she could see amply enough with the lantern.

Four oversized trunks took up considerable space on the floor, and a counter with glass stood against the western wall. Haphazard racks lined the area, and someone had seen fit to freshly paint the walls. Oh, but to have some floral wallpaper or a comfortable fluffy chair for patrons to recline in while they prepared to shop!

As the saying went, there was no time like the present to begin making this the best boutique in Hollow Creek. She laughed to herself. *The only boutique in Hollow Creek.*

Setting the lantern on the counter, she opened the first trunk and gazed upon the lovely merchandise. She held a short-sleeved yellow dress to her bosom and marveled at the ruffled sleeves. She'd owned a similar dress once upon a time.

Next, she lifted two suits and the most elegant cotton blouse with frills, pintucks, and embroidered designs. She draped all of the items over the counter before removing stylish hats and an Irish corset. Ideas overfilled her mind. A string could be stretched from wall to wall on the south side to hang the hosiery, and she would arrange the shoes just so on one of the trunks.

Perhaps she ought to sleep here amongst the fripperies. She involved herself in her endeavors, and sometime later figured it best to return to the apartment lest she truly did fall asleep in her new place of employment.

One of the dresses had lost a button, and upon scouring the trunk, McKenna located it. She'd take it to the apartment and repair it tonight before returning tomorrow. Perhaps she could try a few of the dresses on as well. She'd always adored clothes, and it wouldn't hurt one bit to know how they fit should a customer inquire as such.

Heaving an armload of dresses, suits, and blouses, she opened the door and stepped into the cool night. However what happened next was not something she could have ever anticipated, and she jumped when an abrupt voice called out to her.

One of Sheriff Clayton Beringer's least favorite tasks was the nightly rounds. Thankfully he lived above the barbershop and could eat supper first. Crime, while it did occur, was far rarer in Hollow Creek County than in some areas. For that Clayton was grateful. Most of the arrests consisted of disorderly conduct, drunkenness, saloon fights, petty theft, bribery, and vagrancy. However, he'd unfortunately had to investigate four assaults and a murder in his short tenure.

He peered in the windows of the local businesses as he wandered down the boardwalk. The two saloons in town competed over who could be the rowdiest. Tonight, given the thunderous shouts of men behind the swinging doors and the rackety music and off-key singing, Wulf's Saloon won the contest.

He came upon the empty building his deputy said was intended to be a new millinery and observed a light inside. When he cupped his hands and peered inside, he noticed a woman gathering clothing items.

Who was she and what was she doing?

He hid behind the corner of the building and waited.

Soon, just as he suspected, she emerged with a handful of clothes in her arms.

His first robbery from a business.

And it was a woman.

Clayton inwardly groaned and stalked toward her. His first time ever arresting a woman. But he had to do so. To make Pa proud and to prove to the residents of Hollow Creek he was worthy of the position.

No, no matter what the scenario, he couldn't fail at his new role as sheriff of Hollow Creek County.

"Hold it right there," he said, his voice sounding more like a hiss than an authoritative command from a lawman.

The woman pivoted and stared at him. Would she attempt to make a getaway with the goods? He peered from his side-eye. Did she have a horse waiting for her? An automobile? A fellow robber?

None that he could see.

"I'm going to have to arrest you for thievery."

Her eyes widened. "Absolutely not!" Her tone remained low, and he appreciated that since causing a ruckus at this time of the night wouldn't be the best course of action. Not that they could compete with Wulf's Saloon.

"I'll need you to put those items back in the building from where you took them."

"Took them?" Her eyes rounded. "I did not *take* them."

"Sure looks like it to me." Why else would she be out here under the cloak of darkness with an armload of clothes?

"If I planned to enter the boutique with ill intent and to steal clothes, why would I have a key?" She held up the key and tapped her foot.

"You probably stole that too."

"Stole the key?"

Clayton nodded toward the door of the building she previously exited and gently nudged her. All the while, she complained about someone named Julia. Hadn't Pa always said those who bent the law were fond of shifting the blame on someone else?

The woman set the clothes on a trunk inside the disorderly millinery. He then placed his hand on her arm and escorted her the short distance to the jail.

The woman's profile, with her jaw set firm and her eyes narrowed, told him all he needed to know.

She was not happy at being caught.

Well, who would be? All of those criminals Pa arrested contributed to his earning the Lawman of the Year Award six years in a row. No one wanted to be arrested. But you break the law, you do the time. Simple as that.

Now all these years later, long after losing Pa, Clayton was determined to be as good of a lawman as his father.

A chip off the old block as the saying went.

Except it would take a lot more than arresting a woman stealing clothes for him to be thought of as an effective sheriff in Hollow Creek County.

The woman dragged her feet and pootled along, all the while prattling more nonsense—which Clayton ignored—until they finally reached the jail. He grappled for the keys in his pocket, opened the cell door, and ushered her in.

The light from the lantern and the copper lamp illuminated her face. Her expression went from one of confusion to one of anger in a span of one second.

He closed the door.

"There has been some mistake."

Didn't all criminals claim something similar?

When Clayton first became a sheriff on January 1, 1912, there had been immense satisfaction in closing the cell door with a bang, locking disorderly individuals, drunkards, and the like behind bars, and keeping the public safe.

But this woman looked no more a threat to the public than his own ma. So instead, he closed the cell door lightly rather than clanging it, locked it, then grabbed his chair, flipped it around, and sat backward on it facing her.

"I'll be back in the morning."

"You cannot leave me here."

"There'll be no stealing in my town." There. He said it. Pa would be proud.

"I was *not* stealing."

"Looked that way to me."

The woman clenched her jaw. "You best release me at once or I'll have your job."

The town would have his job if he allowed a robber to get away with the deed.

And Pa?

God rest his soul, Clayton ached to make him proud.

"Sorry, ma'am, I can't do that. You were caught stealing from the new millinery."

"Boutique."

"Boutique?"

The woman huffed, her shoulders rising, then falling. "Yes, boutique."

Clayton shrugged. Millinery, boutique. No difference to him.

CHAPTER TWO

CLAYTON COULDN'T VERY WELL just leave the lady in jail overnight, despite his mention of doing so. Not with old man Swett, the town drunkard, in the cell beside her.

As if sensing Clayton spoke of him, the drunk released a loud and obnoxious snore that reminded Clayton of a train struggling up the tallest mountain in Montana. The snore even ended with a wheezing whistle.

Granted, Swett would be sleeping off his liquor for the duration. But still...

Although tired from a full day of lawman duties, Clayton would do the gentlemanly thing. He'd stay in the sheriff's office overnight, and in the morning, they'd sort out what needed to be settled about the woman's thievery.

Had Pa ever dealt with having to arrest a woman? Clayton plopped into his chair and propped his feet up on the desk. From his side eye, he noticed the woman watching him.

A beautiful woman with her striking blue eyes and coiffed blonde hair. But being a criminal wasn't dependent on whether one was pretty or homely. That much he knew. And why wasn't she sitting on the cot like most prisoners did?

"Ma'am, feel free to take a seat," he said.

"You're incorrect in your arrest," she answered.

Well, they would see about that. No one broke into a business at ten at night—conveniently waiting for darkness to befall the town and for no one to be around before engaging in nefarious activities. Not on his watch. Besides, he had a lot to prove to the town of Hollow Creek. They'd graciously elected him sheriff over that scoundrel, Rantz, and they depended on him to protect the town in which they resided. Clayton wasn't a native of the town, nor had he grown up here, but instead in the neighboring county of Cullman. But when Sheriff Keats left town for a position in Kalispell, that left this position open. Clayton much preferred running for sheriff in Cullman County and following in Pa's footsteps, but the sheriff there did a right fine job.

And Hollow Creek needed him.

Poor millinery owner. Just moved in and already the bandits targeted it.

"Sir..."

She didn't have the voice of a robber, but Clayton surmised an outlaw's voice came in all kinds of tones and pitches. "Yes, ma'am?"

"Please release me immediately."

For someone so confident in their innocence, her voice wavered and for a moment he felt pity for her. Then tossed that notion aside. Pa would have been fair in his assessments, but not a fool. "The judge will see you tomorrow, provided we can schedule a time."

"The judge?"

He nodded. "What is your name, ma'am?"

"Miss McKenna Chapman."

"Well, Miss Chapman, I suggest you make yourself comfortable. The courthouse doesn't open until morning, and that's a few hours away yet."

"But you don't understand."

Didn't all prisoners say much the same? He attempted to get comfortable and willed his eyes to stay open. No sense in falling asleep at his desk. That wouldn't do. He thumbed through the wanted posters on his desk, stood and replaced a few of the older ones on the wall, and returned to his seat. It was now 10:30. Only eight hours or so to go before one of his deputies relieved him. He stretched his arms overhead and closed his eyes for exactly two seconds. Clayton organized the two pencils on his desk, rearranged the stationary he used to write notes, and dusted a few cookie crumbs onto the floor. It was then that he noticed a newspaper tucked on the barrel near the pot-bellied stove. Perhaps it was an issue he hadn't yet read. He shrugged and willed his fatigued legs to wander to the stove to retrieve the paper.

Sitting down a third time, he flipped open the month-old *Hollow Creek Times* and squinted at the words with tired eyes in the glow of the copper lamp on the desk. Advertisements from the mercantile dotted the page—a new couch for ten dollars, men's trousers on sale for two dollars instead of the regular price of four dollars, and ninety-eight pounds of Dakota Flour for $3.25. Calicos and gingham fabric were also on sale for five cents a yard.

He rummaged through the wanted adverts, plentiful advertisements for medicines, including liver pills from some drug store in Illinois, and help for constipation using Syrup of Figs from a California druggist for fifty cents a bottle, postage paid. On the front page, which he'd initially skipped, Clayton read through the news of the town, his attention drawn to one tidbit of information in particular.

Hollow Creek Welcomes New Businesses

Hollow Creek is growing in population and in businesses! Next month, we will welcome two new companies. The first is a dentist, Dr. Molar—yes, that is his real name—who hails from Wisconsin. Dr. Molar will provide superior dental care, including the removal of rotten teeth. He has twelve years of experience and offers to treat teeth with painless methods and without the questionable procedures sometimes used. He will bring all the benefits of a big city dentist to our small town, including porcelain crowns for four dollars, suction teeth for five dollars a set—ones guaranteed not to slip and guaranteed for twenty years—and fillings for fifty cents.

A picture of Dr. Molar graced the page beside the article. Clayton hadn't yet met the dentist, but he had seen him once or twice in town.

He took a drink of his cold coffee as his gaze traveled to the second paragraph about new businesses. This one, albeit not one he would regularly read were it not for boredom, caused him considerable concern.

The other new business is one most women will be euphoric to discover. Some may have noticed numerous clothing trunks delivered and placed inside the former empty building on Main Street. It is about to be empty no longer! Miss Julia Mathilda's Fine Dresses will open in one month with Miss McKenna Chapman as the proprietress of this fine establishment. Hailing from Missoula, her objective will be to provide high-society clothing choices for the stylish Hollow Creek Woman with many wares shipped from Boston, New York, Minneapolis, and Chicago. There will be a special on women's suits for only $12.50 while supplies last. Other items for sale include hats, handbags, necklaces, blouses, shirtwaists, dresses—both long-sleeved and short-sleeved—and corsets.

Miss McKenna Chapman? He sputtered as the distasteful coffee flew from his mouth. With his shirt sleeve, he wiped off the desk and then stood and faced his newest inmate. She rose from the cot where she'd finally plunked herself after his suggestion to make herself comfortable. "Did you say your name is Miss McKenna Chapman?"

"Yes, Sheriff, I did." Even the glow of the copper lamp, he could see her mouth pursed in a straight line. She'd placed her hands on her slender hips and narrowed her eyes at him.

"The Miss McKenna Chapman from Missoula?"

"Indeed," she said between gritted teeth.

"The one who is opening the millinery?"

"Boutique, yes."

He ran a hand through his hair. "Well, I reckon you may be correct."

"About my name or being the one opening the boutique?" Her chilly tone indicated she was not amused.

"Uh, yes, both, and the fact you shouldn't be here."

He broke his eye contact with her and pondered how he might right a severe error in judgment.

Miss Chapman crossed her arms, frowned at him, and tapped her toe, as if waiting for him to humble himself and admit his blunder. And release her. Clayton cleared his throat. "I—uh, well..." he rubbed the back of his neck then snagged the keys and unlocked the lock to her cell.

"What about me? I work at the millinery," mumbled Swett, his jumbled words echoing in the room from where he sprawled on the cot.

"You aren't going anywhere, and you don't work at the millinery. Matter of fact, you don't work at all. As for you, Miss Chapman, I offer my sincerest apologies." He held open the cell door as she stumbled out. Clayton hastily grabbed her arm to steady her. "Are you all right?"

"Besides being locked into a cold and dank jail cell for absolutely no reason in the late evening, oh, yes, I'm just fine." Her last word seethed and matched the glare she offered him. She wrested from his grasp and smoothed her skirt with trembling hands.

"Yes, ma'am, I can see why you are not thrilled at the moment. I truly did believe you were stealing from the new store, and we can't have thievery in Hollow Creek." He cleared his throat again. "Anyhow, reckon I'll accompany you home and let you commence with your evening." Clayton felt like a cad. Not only had he arrested an innocent person—a woman, no less—but he'd ignored her pleas of innocence. The town and the voters would not be appreciative of such a serious mistake.

"I am just fine on my own." Miss Chapman stomped toward the door.

"With all respect, ma'am, it's not safe for you to walk alone this time of night."

"Humph."

That one word said a multitude, and Clayton ought to just allow her to go on her way, but a gentleman—which he prided himself in being—would see to it that she returned home safely.

He pocketed the cell keys lest Swett's unruly friends attempt to sneak in and free him, and offered his elbow.

She rejected it.

That was fine by him. He'd just follow her to wherever she was going, all the while surveilling the area for lawless individuals like the ones who frequented the saloon until all hours of the night or who loomed in the shadows looking to commit crimes.

Two men staggered along the boardwalk, cussing and shoving each other. The moonlight allowed Clayton to notice Miss Chapman flinch, and he hurried along beside her. "Where is it you live, ma'am?"

"Above the boutique," she whispered.

Definitely not a place for her to travel to by her lonesome in the dark. One had to traipse to the back of the building to access that apartment. Not a good idea when who knows what could be lurking in the darkness.

"Well, what do we gots here? You're a right fine pretty lady." One of the men by the name of Sappenfield said as they passed.

Miss Chapman startled and clutched Clayton's arm. He straightened his posture and rested his hand on the gun in his holster. Sappenfield was known for causing trouble and had done jail time for assaulting a lawman in Powell County. "Not your concern. Get home or I'll arrest you for disturbing the peace."

Sappenfield chortled but went on his way with the other man. Clayton kept his attention on both of them. No sense in having his back to those who might seek to do Miss Chapman or him harm.

Pa's face flashed through his mind. He'd died in the line of duty at the hands of a wanted criminal.

With difficulty, he shoved the painful memory aside and steered Miss Chapman to the alleyway. The steep steps leading to the apartment were poorly illuminated, and he wished he'd brought along a lantern. "I'll assist you to your door," he said, gesturing for her to go ahead of him up the stairs. She gripped the railing and took the steps slowly. He followed, keeping an eye on their surroundings. So far, a cat slinking through the alley was the only thing that caught his attention.

At the top of the stairs, he heard her fumble with the key to the door. "Can I assist you?"

This close, he could see that she shivered, and he regretted keeping her out in the chill of the night. She handed him the key, which he deposited into the door and opened for her before returning the key.

"Again, ma'am, I do apologize."

She said nothing, only stepped inside and closed the door behind him. He stood on the landing, briefly scanning through the darkness. Regret tightened his chest and he doubted that, although weariness overwhelmed every part of him, he'd get no shut-eye tonight.

Chapter Three

MCKENNA REMOVED HER SHOES and collapsed onto her bed, her heart racing in her chest. Never had she ever imagined she'd spend time in jail. Of course, Father hadn't foreseen that either when he was arrested that day.

Her arms shook as she attempted to find comfort on the thin mattress. How long had she been held captive in the dank cell? An hour? And to think Father could be in jail for months, if not years. Or even sent to the prison in Deer Lodge.

She shivered and tugged the blanket up to her chin. Tears breached her eyelids and a sob built in her throat. Sleep would not come easily tonight, that much she knew.

That horrid sheriff ought to be ashamed of himself for arresting an innocent woman. His time was better served capturing criminals not those who merely wanted to begin their new employ as the manager of a boutique.

McKenna had anticipated a lot of things when first learning she would be living in Hollow Creek. She'd expected to be frustrated at the thought of residing in an uncivilized and backward town after spending her entire life in a cultured city. She'd known it would take time to adjust to the lack of amenities and the unsophisticated lifestyle she would now find herself.

But she hadn't expected to be arrested and led to the town jail by a man whom she now determined to be her sworn enemy.

The following day, McKenna carried the armload of clothes back down the stairs of the apartment and to the boutique. She'd spent the morning after a fitful night fixing the button on the dress and trying on a few of the other items.

She yawned. If only her night hadn't been so fitful. But then, being arrested wasn't a common occurrence, and sleeping in a new place hadn't been conducive to restful slumber either.

As she rounded the corner and stepped up onto the boardwalk, she noticed just ahead none other than that daft sheriff sweeping the walkway, his back to her. But goodness. Didn't the man have better things to do with his time? Like arrest innocent people? McKenna shuffled the clothes so they wouldn't drag on the ground and gave the man a wide berth as she prepared to pass him on the way to the shop.

With a grandiose movement, he arched the broom and an enormous plume of dirt and debris engulfed her. She choked as the rubble plunked her on the cheek, and she swiftly angled herself away from what could very well ruin the merchandise.

"Oh, sorry about that. I didn't see you there."

"How could you not see me there?" McKenna edged a shoulder to her cheek in an effort to wipe away and remove some of the dust.

"On the contrary, Miss..."

"Chapman. The one you arrested last night, remember? *Falsely* arrested."

The man blinked slowly. Had he already forgotten his faux pas? "Oh, yes, I remember. Sorry, Miss Chapman. For that and for sweeping the dirt your way. My back was to you, and I was just trying to get this done in as efficient a manner as possible."

To his credit, the sheriff did appear stunned that he swept up a good lot of rubble in her direction. Still. "Yes, well, perhaps you ought to watch what you're doing."

21

The man propped the broom against the building. "Here. Allow me to assist you with those clothes."

Aunt Julia Mathilda would experience vapors if she knew McKenna was handing off the boutique's precious wares to a man who likely had filthy hands.

"No thank you."

"Suit yourself." He shook his head. "You go along and pass by, and I'll wait until you are in the millinery before I start sweeping again."

"Boutique. It is far more exquisite than a millinery. Julia Mathilda's Fine Dresses carries only the grandest, premier, first-class clothing shipped all the way from Boston, New York, Chicago, and Minneapolis."

The sheriff chuckled. It was a nice chuckle, but then, rabble-rousers could have nice laughs, she supposed. "Who cares where it came from?"

She frowned, regretting the fleeting thought that he had a nice chuckle. "Well, those with good taste do."

"I don't care at all about where my shirts, boots, and hat come from or whether my jeans were shipped from a city. For all I care, they could have been made right here in Hollow Creek."

"Yes, and that is apparent, sir."

His mouth fell open. Had her insult been effective? She suddenly felt smug and jutted her chin. "Now, if you'll excuse me, I have things to do."

This time, he stepped out of her way and allowed the wide berth. She perfected her posture and added determination to her steps. It was good to be out of his presence, but why then did she feel the urge to take a peek—just a teeny tiny peek—behind her to see his reaction?

McKenna nonchalantly peered over her shoulder. He was staring at her, or at least in her direction. Heat suffused her face, although she had no explanation for it.

It was in that brief moment when her head was turned, that she tumbled off the side of the boardwalk. Her ankle gave way, and she tottered, mindful of the expensive clothes in her arms before she landed in a heap.

Ma didn't need to have instilled in him the necessity of always being a gentleman for him to know he ought to assist Miss Chapman in her sorry state.

"Ma'am, are you all right?" He offered a hand and was surprised when she took it. Gently, so as not to topple her off her feet again, he righted her.

She offered him the crustiest glower he'd ever seen, and he'd seen a lot of crusty glowers being a sheriff and all.

Without another word, Miss Chapman brushed past him, her arms overloaded with the garments, now haphazard and soiled.

Clayton finished sweeping—a task that wasn't his favorite—before checking on his prisoners and tending to other duties. At noon, he strolled to Dell's Mercantile to purchase a few provisions for his noonday meal. Vera, Thad and Emilie Evanson's hired help, was in the store chatting with Reverend Arkley and Mrs. Dell, who owned the mercantile with her husband.

And Miss Chapman was in the corner perusing baking items.

Regrettably, he needed to snatch some canned peaches, which were next to the flour and sugar.

"Sheriff, how are you today?" Vera turned from prattling on with Reverend Arkley and Mrs. Dell.

He jerked his head up from the shelf with the peaches. So much for attempting to go unnoticed by Miss Chapman.

"Hello, Vera. I'm doing well. You?"

"Wonderful. Say, have you met our newest resident?"

Clayton looked around him, hoping Vera wasn't referring to Miss Chapman. But who else could it be? Reverend Arkley had lived here forever and Mrs. Dell's family founded the town. "Uh, who?"

Vera sidled up alongside him. "McKenna, dear, allow me to introduce you to Reverend Arkley and Mrs. Dell."

The three exchanged pleasantries before the pastor and mercantile owner continued their conversation.

"And have you met Sheriff Beringer?" Vera asked Miss Chapman.

"Unfortunately, yes." She arched an eyebrow at him.

Vera held a hand to her chest. "But goodness, that sounds ominous."

"Indeed, it is."

Those pretty blue eyes of hers stared right into his soul. "We have met," he confirmed in response to Vera's inquiry.

After several seconds ticked by, the older woman again spoke. "Well, I best bid you both farewell."

"So long, Vera. Nice to see you again." Miss Chapman continued examining the baked goods. He noticed she had some dirt crusted on her left cheek and her hair was in slight disarray. Her black skirt was splotched with a few sections of dust, as was her yellow blouse. It was then that he noticed he was staring and quickly averted his gaze. Yes, she was a comely woman but uppity and snobbish.

And he for certain wouldn't let her know he found her to be comely.

Over the next two days, McKenna continued to unpack and organize the merchandise. She would be ready to open the boutique in a week, just as Aunt Julia Mathilda wanted. A knock at the door sounded, and she peered up from her duties to see a young boy.

So far, only a handful of townsfolk attempted to peer into the shop, most likely out of curiosity. McKenna reassured them she wasn't taking customers just yet, but would be soon, and for them to hurry back without haste for the first day of opening when women's suits would be on a fabulous sale. She hurried to the door and opened it. "May I help you?"

"Yes, ma'am, just handing out these here papers." He took one from his plentiful stack and offered it to her.

"Thank you." McKenna closed the door behind the boy and read the notice.

The spur from Bleakney to Hollow Creek is just about complete! In two days, one will no longer have to find alternate routes of transport but can board the train and travel in comfort by rail. In celebration, we will be offering tickets to Bleakney and Missoula at half price for the next five days. For more information or to secure your tickets, please visit the new depot at the corner of Main Street and Fourth.

Her spirits buoyed. What if...

Of course, she would have to see if she had sufficient funds, but wouldn't it be delightful to travel to Bleakney to see Father for the first time in months? Would the jail allow visitors? And then to continue to Missoula and visit with Mother and Arrosa for two days before returning for the boutique's opening? She already missed them so very much, and this would afford her some time with them before things became hectic at the shop and the price for a train ticket was well beyond her means.

With renewed excitement, McKenna went about her tasks with the plan of securing a train ticket tomorrow and traveling to Missoula in the next couple of days. She strung a line across the shop from one end to the other directly in front of the door. She'd move the one end later to its permanent place once she assured herself her plan would work.

Then she clipped the hosiery to the line.

It was sometime later that she noticed Sheriff Beringer peering into the boutique. Whatever was he doing?

His nose was pressed against the window and his eyes darted about. McKenna respected him because he was a lawman, but that didn't mean she had to like him. He opened the door and walked right into the hosiery McKenna just finished hanging. The sheriff shoved aside the stocking that attached itself to his face.

"May I help you?"

"Yes. Are there any criminals hiding in here?"

"No criminals here." *Well, except for the one you wrongly arrested who is not a criminal.* She was appalled at his inquiry, to say the least. "First you arrested me even though I was innocent, and not, in fact, stealing from my own shop, and now you ask if I am harboring a criminal?"

"Not what I intended by that question, ma'am." He scanned the room. "Please lock the door after I leave."

"I beg your pardon?"

"We have an escaped prisoner on the loose, and I don't want him to attempt to hide in here."

Without another word, he turned on his heel and left.

Terror zipped through her. The seriousness in his tone took her aback, and she watched as he strode down the boardwalk with purpose. Townsfolk scurried inside buildings, and McKenna locked the door as the sheriff had requested.

Having lived in Missoula with a population of over 12,000 her entire life, McKenna knew crime abounded, but never had she had to worry. Living in the high-society part of town afforded her family luxuries beyond those that were monetary.

Not ten minutes later, a man bolted out of nowhere and down Main Street. She could hear his footsteps thumping on the boardwalk. His eyes met hers when he stopped in front of the boutique and tried the doorknob before banging on the door. The hairs lifted on the back of her neck and her chest tightened with panic. Sheriff Beringer and two other men, one of whom she presumed to be a lawman, apprehended the outlaw from behind and hauled him away. A few minutes later, the sound of a gunshot cracked the air.

She drew in a lungful of air and attempted to quell her shaky breath. What if the sheriff hadn't warned her to lock the door?

At half past two, a group of people had gathered at the Hollow Creek Courthouse at the edge of town where Sheriff Beringer would relay a statement. McKenna stood behind the crowd of whispering townsfolk, and the sheriff stood on the steps of the brick building.

A man McKenna had not yet met in a suit and fedora addressed the crowd. "Ladies and gentlemen, Sheriff Beringer has a statement to make regarding the capture of Devon Hagge. Sheriff."

The sheriff scanned the faces before commencing. "Thank you for meeting here today. Devon Hagge was being transported from a town in the southeastern portion of our county to Deer Lodge to do his time for killing two lawmen, assaulting multiple individuals, horse thievery, and robbing several banks in Montana and Idaho. He was heavily protected since he'd already escaped once."

Those in attendance gasped, and McKenna held a hand to her chest, hoping to settle her racing heartbeat.

"We received news that Hagge had escaped and was headed this way to locate his brother who formerly resided in the area. After we captured him, he attempted to shoot a member of our posse and lost his life."

McKenna's heart settled in her throat. If Father was sentenced to Deer Lodge, would he be forced to interact with heartless criminals like Devon Hagge?

CHAPTER FOUR

THE MAN AT THE ticket counter of the newly completed depot handed McKenna her train ticket. If the railroad wasn't offering a half-price discount to encourage folks to use the brand-new spur, McKenna would never have been able to afford it.

Not with the necessity of saving all of her income just to keep Mother and Arrosa from being homeless and providing for Arrosa's continual medical care.

Not that she minded, for she didn't. She'd walk to the East Coast and back with nary a rest for her family.

McKenna boarded the six a.m. train a few moments later. Excited voices clamored above the usual train noises from the passengers—some of whom had never before boarded such a mode of transport. For McKenna, however, this was far from the first time. She'd ridden trains all over the United States and even some in Europe.

Those days were far in the past now.

She folded her hands in her lap and peered out the window. In the crowd, she noted that irritating Sheriff Beringer conversing with a man she recognized as the hardware store's owner. He looked in her direction at that moment, an expression she couldn't discern crossing his face.

McKenna inwardly shrugged. The man was an oddity and a daft one at that. What he thought of her was of no consequence.

However, while he had unfairly arrested her, he'd also earned her respect when he'd thwarted Mr. Hagge's plan.

The porter announced his "All Aboard" call, the train whistle blew, and the train advanced to its first destination. When they arrived, McKenna reached for her lone carpetbag and stood in line behind the other passengers.

The only stop before Missoula was in a town called Bleakney. When the spur opened between Hollow Creek and Missoula, the city council in Bleakney persuaded the train's owners to stop in Bleakney to hopefully assist the dying town. McKenna recalled reading about it in the newspaper, and she, just like many did, suspected the town's mayor was a close friend of one of the railroad's owners.

McKenna disembarked for her short visit before the train again continued on its route. Such a stop was more than convenient, and while her next duty was essential, it was not without trepidation.

A tear dampened her cheek, and she swiped it away. He would be happy to see her, that much she knew.

While other passengers ate at the humble restaurant, stayed on the train, or left it entirely as Bleakney was their destination, McKenna strolled down the boardwalk and to the dismal white building with the words Bleakney Jail posted in black lettering.

She inhaled a sharp breath, wrapped her fingers around the carpetbag handle more tightly, and pushed open the door to the jail.

"May I help you, ma'am?" A lawman with a curly gray mustache rose from his desk.

"Yes, sir. I'm here to visit one of your—" her voice faltered. That Father was an inmate caused bile to burn her throat.

"Your name, please."

"McKenna Chapman."

"And the name of the prisoner you'd like to visit?"

"Egbert Chapman."

The man arched a gray eyebrow. "Wait right here."

The interior of the Bleakney Jail was just as bleak—for lack of a better word—as she imagined the jail cells to be—even more so than Hollow Creek's. Wanted posters hung on the otherwise bare walls and a sense of gloom radiated from the dismal room in need of a fresh coat of paint and a new floor.

Poor Father. While this had to be better than the prison in Deer Lodge or even the Missoula County Jail, residing here would be a dreary and miserable experience.

The lawman returned a few seconds later with another officer who led McKenna down a long hall past four cells, two of which housed uncouth men offering crude words and expletives. At the farthest end of a more desolate area of the cell block, he stopped. "You have fifteen minutes," he said.

That was about all the time she would have as the train would be leaving in a half hour and by the time she gathered her wits about her, she'd need to board.

Visiting Father in the cell had to be the worst experience of her life besides seeing Arrosa struggle with her illness.

"Father," she gasped.

He reached through the bars and grasped her hand. "Hello, McKenna." He'd raised his head slightly, but he didn't look her in the eye.

"Father, how—how are you?"

"I'm all right."

But one perusal of his gaunt cheeks and solemn expression indicated he was far from all right.

"Have you heard any news about if they will move you?"

"No. For now, I'll stay here."

McKenna worked her throat through a gritty swallow. "Do you ever get to be outside?"

"I have a window in my cell." Father turned slightly and pointed to what could be described as slightly larger than a crack in the plaster. "They also allow us to go outside from time to time if we've exhibited good behavior."

She knew without a doubt Father would not partake in anything but good behavior.

With the exception of the grave mistake that landed him here in the first place.

He hadn't shaved in a while, and his hairy face took her aback. "Father, please look at me."

He raised his eyes to hers and she saw the shame and guilt in their depths. "How have you been? Have you been to see your mother and Arrosa?"

"I'm on my way now to see them. I've been fine."

"How is Hollow Creek?"

McKenna inclined her head to the side. "Well, let's just say it's an adventure."

"Aren't all things?" Father answered wryly.

She clutched his hand. "I miss you so."

"Before long our family will be together again."

She wanted to ask how he could be so sure but thought better of it. Before all that happened, she and Father had not been particularly close. Egbert Chapman's work had far surpassed family in his life in those days. Yes, he'd always been a good provider, and McKenna and Arrosa knew he loved them, but they didn't spend time together as other fathers and daughters did except for charity events and vacationing each summer at their home in New York.

A home that had long been auctioned off to help repay the debt Father owed.

He tugged his hand away, and she reluctantly let go. "I've been doing a lot of reading," he said and retrieved a Bible from his cot. "Never knew how interesting this could be."

"Do you need other reading material?"

"No. This is what I mainly read. They do have some other books the reverend from one of the churches brings on occasion. Do you remember when we attended church, McKenna?"

"Yes. On Easter and Christmas."

Father nodded and pressed his lips together in a firm line. "If I could, I'd attend more often now."

McKenna wasn't sure she would. After all, hadn't it been the Lord's fault Arrosa became ill?

"Have you been to the church in Hollow Creek?"

"No, not yet."

"Hmm."

The familiar word Father was known for saying while pondering nearly encouraged her to smile. She supposed that with all the changes, some things would remain the same.

"Time is up," called the officer, who leaned against a vacant cell a short distance away.

Father reached for her hand. "I love you, McKenna."

The tears burned her eyes, and she did her best to choke back a sob. "I love you too."

"God will take care of us. We only need to trust."

The words—so foreign both to hear and to hear from Father's mouth—drew her temporarily from her melancholy.

"Ma'am? It's time to go." The officer strode toward her, a flash of kindness in his dark eyes.

"I'll visit again, Father."

"Please tell your mother and Arrosa hello."

"I will."

He nodded and waved as McKenna stumbled through the gloomy hall and back to the front area of the jail.

Just as she exited the building, she heard the train whistle, and she launched into a brisk walk. To miss the train to Missoula would not do, for she hadn't the additional funds to waste.

"All aboard!"

Bleakney was a small town, smaller than Hollow Creek, but it might as well have been a sizable, thriving city for the length of time it took McKenna to rush from the jail to the depot. "Wait!" she cried, her voice desperate and competing with the occasional automobile, a wagon, and other clamor. "Please wait!" Slow-moving individuals on the boardwalk in front of her restricted her progress. "Excuse me, please. Excuse me."

The young couple either didn't hear her or ignored her for they remained in place. McKenna haphazardly stepped off the side of the boardwalk, her ankle twisting as she did so. Pain shot through her foot. But there wasn't time to nurse her injury. She waved frantically in the direction of the train. "I'm coming! Please wait!"

Being stranded in a foreign town was not her idea of a pleasurable way to spend the afternoon, and who knew when the next train would leave for Missoula if she missed this one?

Her ankle ached but she pressed on. If only the train would wait another minute...

Ahead, a grocery store had decided to set a stand of goods on the boardwalk, causing a narrow passageway. Mindful of stepping cautiously off the side this time, McKenna did so, only to see an out-of-control wagon heading her way at the last minute. She leaped back onto the boardwalk just as a plume of dust rose in the air. Folks were so careless. At least if they could afford themselves an automobile, they could control it more easily than a wagon.

As soon as the thought entered her mind, she shoved it aside. Her family could no longer afford the necessities of life, let alone an automobile. The days of Sunday drives through the country and picnics in the mountains while Father drove the motorcar were far in the past.

Out of breath, she finally reached the depot just as the train began to move along the tracks. "Sir! Please, I need to board!"

Had the conductor even seen her?

But just as she was about to surrender to staying in Bleakney and wasting her precious earnings on an unnecessary train ticket, the train slowed to a stop, and the conductor motioned for her to approach.

"Thank you so much." McKenna stumbled up the steps and into the train. Her eyes filmed with unshed tears, and her weakened knees barely allowed her to stagger to the first available seat several rows back. Her heartbeat pulsed wildly in her chest as she reclined and closed her eyes.

A short while later, Missoula came into view. The Northern Pacific Railway Depot bustled with those both arriving and preparing to leave. She gingerly stepped from the train, mindful of her injured ankle, and plopped on a bench in front of the looming orange-brick building. She'd rest a mere minute or two before the walk into town. McKenna couldn't afford the luxury of boarding a streetcar or borrowing some other mode of transport.

She inhaled, then exhaled, the plans for the remainder of the day forming in her mind. She would stay in Missoula with Mother and Arrosa today and tomorrow. The following day she would return to Hollow Creek with whatever new dresses Aunt Julia Mathilda requested she take.

Finally, after several minutes, she gathered her composure and started the lengthy distance to her destination. After some time, the pain in her ankle eased a bit, for which she was grateful. She passed by Aunt Julia Mathilda's, and for a moment contemplated asking her aunt if she'd deliver her to Mother's apartment, but then thought better of it. While she loved her relative, Aunt Julia Mathilda had been quite clear that she'd not have much to do with McKenna's family after Father's crime.

"For propriety's sake," Aunt Julia Mathilda had said. "I can't allow anything to mar the reputation of the business I have put my heart and soul into all these years."

Indeed. For McKenna's aunt, her livelihood trumped even family.

Not that McKenna didn't understand, for she did. If folks—especially those of higher society—became aware that Aunt Julia Mathilda was related to a thief, they would be less inclined to spend their dollars at her boutique.

McKenna swallowed the difficult realization that once upon a time she, too, would have put monetary value over family.

The abundance of traffic on the busy streets sharply contrasted with the more relaxed atmosphere in Hollow Creek. The hubbub and commotion of her surroundings caused her to realize something she never before would have imagined.

After a short time of residing there, McKenna Chapman much preferred Hollow Creek.

Several blocks later, her legs aching and her ankle screaming for rest, McKenna entered the outskirts of the main part of the city. She pivoted down Heersink Avenue and continued for what seemed an endless amount of time before turning one last time onto Thorburn Street. The farther along she proceeded down

Thorburn, the more her surroundings changed until she entered the undesirable Thorburn Flats. No more the classy city streets of her beloved town. Instead, the scene before her reminded her of photographs of the tenements in New York. Structures rose against the skyline with clotheslines strung across apartment buildings, filthy streets, and a beggar or two on the corner.

The very last building in Thorburn Flats was the one she sought. A dilapidated dark-orange brick building with a dingy exterior greeted her. Dirty windows, a few of them broken and boarded, and crumbling steps inside reminded her of how far her family had fallen.

A wave of emotion clouded her vision as she limped up the seven steps to the porch and entered through the door, up another staircase to the top floor, and finally to room twelve. She knocked twice before Mother answered.

"Hello, Mother."

"McKenna!"

Mother opened her arms, and McKenna wasted no time flying into them. Before all that had happened, she could count the times on one hand that Mother enveloped her in a hug. Now in recent months, she'd lost the ability to compute the countless times. Arrosa's illness and their family's recent downfall had drawn them closer together.

McKenna clung to her mother as the tears slid down her cheeks. Mother held her and patted the back of her head. "Whatever is the matter?"

She took a step back. "I've missed you and Arrosa. And Father."

Mother blinked rapidly. "We've missed you as well." Her brow crinkled. "You are so thin. Have you enough to eat?"

"Yes, more than enough." It was Mother McKenna was worried about. She appeared more frail than she remembered her to be. If Mother knew McKenna set aside nearly all of her pay except the bare minimum she needed for necessities, Mother would have an opinion about that for certain.

Mother seemed satisfied with her answer and reached for McKenna's hand. "Come sit down and tell me how you fare."

McKenna followed her into the shabby abode. No more fine furniture, no more numerous rooms in a mansion that could fit several families comfortably. Instead, dirt crusted the corners of the worn floor, water circles stained the ceiling, and a musty smell filled the room. A makeshift table and two chairs, one with a broken leg, a cot, a potbellied stove for warmth, and an old cooking stove provided the only furniture besides an overturned barrel. Behind a curtain—not even a curtain so much as a piece of fraying dingy fabric—hung from the ceiling and assisted with maintaining some privacy for Arrosa and for anyone wishing to take a bath or use the lavatory.

At least the dilapidated apartment had electricity and running water. That was more than some had.

But substantially less than their mansion in the sophisticated Amwood Heights area where they once resided.

Cleanliness meant much to Mother, but no matter how much she attempted to keep the apartment tidy, it was to no avail with its tattered and threadbare appearance.

She took a seat on the broken chair placed against the wall to keep it from falling over and gestured at Mother to take the other chair. She did so, and McKenna grieved the exhaustion lining her face. Mother's red chapped hands were folded in her lap, and she wore a faded dress that hung from her thin body.

No pearls, no diamond earrings, and no luxurious clothing. Her hair hung in a messy chignon at the nape of her neck, gray-blonde strands escaping and plastering to her cheek. More wrinkles than McKenna recalled from their last meeting creased her face.

But no matter how unpolished Mother appeared, she was still beautiful.

"How are things with the boutique?"

"They're going well. Hollow Creek is small, so I'm sure there will be days when I'll only have one or two customers, if any. But there is an influx of wealthy ranchers in the area, and their wives will no doubt be fond of having a place to shop if they aren't planning a trip to Missoula."

"I'm glad to hear that. Julia Mathilda will be proud."

Mother always did have an overly positive attitude where her sister was concerned. "While it's highly uncivilized and rather primitive, I am growing somewhat fond of the town. Emilie Evanson and her hired help, a woman by the name of Vera, have been so welcoming." McKenna would omit that she had to put on airs with nearly everyone she encountered.

Her mother handed her a cup of water. "I'm sorry I don't have more to drink, but I haven't been to the grocery store this week."

It wasn't that long ago that coffee, tea, hot chocolate, milk, or juice were available for the asking. "It's fine, Mother. I'm rather thirsty, and water is best."

Mother offered a small smile. "It's so good to hear you're doing well."

McKenna finished sipping the beverage and set the chipped cup on the table. "Really, the only impediment is the sheriff."

"The sheriff?" Mother inhaled a sharp breath, and McKenna knew she must assuage her concern lest she relive the day Father was arrested at their former home in broad daylight.

"Not because of any insinuation of a crime committed..." She paused and recalled the annoying man's insistence she was a criminal breaking into the boutique. "Only because the man himself is rather daft."

"A daft sheriff? How did that happen? Were the townsfolk not aware when they voted for him?"

McKenna shrugged. "There could be some in the county who were unaware. I believe him to be a suitable lawman, he's just—shall we say—a vexing individual. A nuisance, an aggravation, and an irritant."

"All of those things?"

"Indeed. But most like him. I believe I'm in the minority."

"Is he an older gentleman?"

"I would surmise a year or two older than myself."

Mother's brow furrowed. "Well, be that as it may, I do hope he doesn't attempt to be a bother."

Sheriff Clayton Beringer already was a bother, but she'd not elaborate, especially about her unfortunate time spent in jail and the frightening episode with the escaped prisoner. Mother had enough to worry about.

When she retrieved McKenna's cup, McKenna again noticed Mother's blistered hands. "I was thinking I might move back to Missoula so I can assist you with housecleaning and Arrosa. With the both of us..."

"Absolutely not."

"Begging your pardon?"

"While we both miss you something terrible, you will not move back here and assist me with housecleaning. Not when you have befitting employment at the boutique. Besides, it would pay far better than anything you could earn cleaning houses."

"But, Mother, it would be easier if I were here. It would alleviate some of the burden you endure having to live here..." McKenna gestured, palms up, while she scanned the room.

"Having to live here, work at a job that is tiring and below your station, and having to take care of Arrosa."

"Below my station?"

"I only meant—"

Mother pursed her lips. "I'll have you know that I am grateful for the housecleaning jobs. Were it not for those, I'm not sure how we would survive since I no longer have the laundress position."

"I'm only saying that I could relieve you of some of your duties by working alongside you at the houses and then assisting with Arrosa."

"If the cleaning positions are below my station, they will be below yours too." Mother folded her arms across her chest and gave McKenna what she and Arrosa termed the "pointy-eye-brow" expression Mother used when she was disappointed, disgruntled, or irritated. In this case, likely disappointed in McKenna's poor choice of verbiage.

"It is below both of our stations, or at least the stations we were accustomed to. Please forgive my prior statement, Mother. I meant no disrespect. You are correct in that were it not for the housecleaning jobs, we wouldn't be able to survive. I am happy to work with you cleaning the houses. We could alternate days so that it wouldn't be so grueling for you." Her gaze darted to Mother's hands.

"I won't allow it, McKenna. You stay at the shop in Hollow Creek."

"When Arrosa heals, you two can move there with me. I live above the shop, and there's room for all of us."

"Arrosa is in no condition to travel and may not be for some time."

McKenna knew both of those things were true, but it hadn't stopped her from thinking about how wonderful it would be for the three of them to be together again until Father was released from jail. She stared at her mother and into the blue eyes so like her own. Years ago when McKenna entered a slightly rebellious phase, she and Mother had not gotten along. Father surmised it was because they were so much alike in character and personality. But in the months since Father's arrest and Arrosa's illness, they'd become closer and had put their differences aside.

"If you are sure you don't want me to move back to Missoula."

"I'm sure. As I mentioned, the pay is better for you, and Julia Mathilda needs your help whether she admits it or not."

McKenna didn't mention that her Aunt Julia Mathilda was quite capable of earning a sufficient living just with her Missoula boutique. "All right then. I will stay where I am." McKenna straightened her posture. "But I insist on something."

The pointy eyebrow emerged again. "And that is?"

"I'd like to assist with Arrosa while I'm here."

"I appreciate that, McKenna. She'll be delighted to see you once she awakens. You had me concerned that your insistence might be far more presumptuous."

"That's only my first insistence. My second being that you take a nice long bath while I make supper."

"You're exhausted from your trip. I'll make *you* supper."

"No, Mother. I insist."

"Well, in that case, all right."

A twinge of guilt overcame McKenna. Mother was clearly fatigued and didn't have the wherewithal to argue. Which would be to McKenna's benefit when she added to her demands.

"On my way from Hollow Creek, I visited Father, and tomorrow while I am still here tending to Arrosa, I want you to travel to see him."

"McKenna..."

"Mother..."

Her mother blinked rapidly and held a hand to her mouth. "Have we the funds for me to take the train to see him?"

"We do."

McKenna would figure out the shortfall later.

Mother began to sob then, and McKenna regretted causing her any additional tension. She stood and wrapped her arms around Mother's thin shoulders.

"I have missed him so much."

"I know."

Silent tears rolled down McKenna's face as she continued to hug Mother. "He will be so glad to see you," she whispered.

"I can't help but think of him all alone in that cell. I know it was his fault for what he chose to do, but he did it for us."

"He did."

McKenna gently rubbed Mother's back as she continued to weep. After several minutes, Mother collected herself and dabbed at her eyes with a fisted hand. "Was he all right when you saw him?"

"He was. He said to tell you and Arrosa hello." McKenna debated her next words. "Mother, he has lost weight and his cheeks are sallow, but he's as handsome as he always was."

"He's lost weight? Are they not feeding him?"

"I'm sure he's being fed, but it's not like the food…" no sense in bringing up the lavish meals Cook made for them. "It's not like the food is that tasty as it's likely broth or beans. Father has never cottoned to beans."

"That's the truth." Mother stifled a giggle. "Do you recall that social event that was actually a bean-tasting fundraiser?"

McKenna remembered it well. "Oh, yes. Father insisted we go because all of his coworkers and his boss from the bank were in attendance. We tried to warn him."

"We did indeed. But your father can be a bit, shall we say, bullheaded at times?"

"And when he discovered all manners of beans were all that would be served for the main course, he was forced to subsist by eating only salad, fruits, and desserts."

Mother laughed. "I have never seen someone eat so much lettuce. And drink so much coffee."

"Didn't he have a stomachache from overconsumption of cookies and cake?"

"He did. We heard about it for days. Unfortunately, he overindulged in apples, grapes, and oranges as well."

They continued to laugh until Mother reached for McKenna's hands. "Thank you for the delightful memory. Delightful for us, although not so delightful for your father."

That caused them to laugh again, and McKenna reveled in the release of stress from the past several months.

"Let's bring Arrosa out here so you can take a bath while I prepare supper."

"All right." Mother stood. "You know, I was thinking just this morning that the Lord has been so faithful to us."

"The Lord?"

"Yes. Granted, I know we only attended church on Easter and Christmas, but I've been learning more about Him from one of the ladies I clean for. She's constantly reading the Bible, and then while I dust the mantle and sweep the floors, she'll tell me what she's read. I truly had no idea about all she's told me." Mother tapped her chin. "She said the Lord is faithful. I didn't think so at first. After all, look at the predicament we have found ourselves in. But then as I walked home that night, I thought of how we have a roof over our heads to keep us from the inclement weather. While not plentiful, we do have food. You and I both have jobs, and Arrosa hasn't gotten any worse. She's still with us." At the last sentence, Mother's voice broke. "I do believe it is true that the Lord is faithful."

McKenna knew little about the Lord and whether or not He was faithful, but she did have to admit Mother had a point. And far be it from her to argue if it was something that gave her mother peace.

CHAPTER FIVE

"MCKENNA, IS THAT YOU?" A soft voice interrupted her and Mother's conversation.

McKenna rose and tugged the curtain aside. Arrosa rested on the narrow bed and attempted to prop herself on an elbow but failed. "You came." Not even the pain she so obviously endured disguised the joy in Arrosa's countenance.

She took a seat beside Arrosa's bed on a worn two-foot-wide bench and planted a hand on her sister's arm. "How are you feeling?"

Tears dampened Arrosa's long eyelashes and her feet jerked beneath the tattered green quilt. Her hands followed with uncontrollable shaking.

"Are you cold?"

"She has the horrific shakes from time to time," said Mother, her own voice wavering.

"Oh, Arrosa, I'm so sorry."

Before the rheumatic fever took hold of her, Arrosa had never been ill a day in her life with the exception of a gastrointestinal infection when she was three and a bout with the croup as a baby. Yet now, here she was—bedridden. McKenna leaned over and rested her head beside her sister's and wrapped her in a hug. Silent tears rolled down her own cheeks, and she felt the heat emanating from Arrosa due to her burning fever. What had become of her once strong and vivacious sister? Her matted auburn hair hung in clumps at the base of her neck, and her hazel eyes, dull and watery, worried McKenna.

After a few seconds, Arrosa clutched McKenna's arm. "I've missed you so." She blinked rapidly. "How long can you stay?"

If only she could live here with Mother and Arrosa! "I'll be here through tomorrow." McKenna released her hold and sat up straight on the bench.

The letdown on Arrosa's ashen face saddened her. "Are you feeling any better since I last saw you?"

Her sister put a hand on her chest. "The chest pain has worsened, and my joints..." with effort, she pushed up the sleeve of her white nightgown to reveal a swollen wrist. "My ankles and elbows are swollen as well, and the pain is unmanageable. And if only I wasn't so tired all the time."

"That's been the worst," said Mother, squeezing beside McKenna to assist Arrosa to a sitting position so she could sip slowly from a glass. The water dribbled down her chin, and Arrosa attempted to dab at it with an unsteady hand. McKenna spied a handkerchief on the shelf above Arrosa's bed, and she grasped it and dabbed at first Arrosa's tears, then her chin.

Mother moved aside and perched on the end of Arrosa's bed. Her voice shook as she spoke. "We'll need to check your rash again." She gently pushed up Arrosa's sleeves to reveal a red rash. She then swiftly removed the blanket to Arrosa's bare legs peeping beneath her gown. They, too, were covered in a rash as well as other peculiar bumps.

Her sister shivered, and Mother hastily returned the covers and tucked her in more tightly. "I'm so cold, Mother."

"I'll gather my coat."

Mother stood but returned seconds later with her coat—a piece of clothing that at one time had been of the most expensive quality. Father purchased it for her from Aunt Julia Mathilda's boutique along with at least three trunkfuls of other elegant clothes. Mother pressed the coat along Arrosa's sides, and her gaze darted in the direction of the fireplace with its meager stack of logs.

No one should need a fire on this pleasant June day, and McKenna reasoned that Mother wouldn't even consider such a prospect were it not for Arrosa's fever-induced chills. "It's a challenge," said Mother. "If we cover her with more blankets and coats and light the fire, her fever will increase. But I can't stand the thought of her being cold." She wrung her hands.

They carefully pushed the wheeled bed outside of the curtained area to give Mother privacy. While Mother took a bath, McKenna searched for enough food in the cupboards and the ice box to make a substantial meal. Such was not the case. A loaf of bread, some preserves, four eggs, a pitcher of water, some crackers, and a few miscellaneous cans of food were the only items in the house. Mother insisted it was because she hadn't the opportunity to go the grocery store. McKenna pondered if this was how they always lived—with only scant food items at any given time.

"I'll be visiting the grocer tomorrow as well," Mother had said. But her words had not sounded convincing, and once again guilt threatened to smother McKenna. How could she leave her mother and sister in such abject poverty? Tomorrow after she paid a visit to Aunt Julia Mathilda's, she'd find a way to secure more food than what her measly pay would afford.

After a paltry supper of bread and two eggs shared between the three of them, Arrosa again fell asleep.

"Mother, you shouldn't have to carry this burden alone." Thank goodness she'd drawn a wage while preparing to manage the shop.

"I'm not. If it weren't for the money you send us from Julia Mathilda's shop—" Mother's chin trembled. She'd never known hunger and poverty as she did now. McKenna recalled her speaking about her life as a child and never having a want. That extended into her adulthood until recently. If only her parents hadn't misused their finances. If only Father hadn't embezzled. If only Arrosa hadn't become ill. If only they hadn't lost everything.

The culmination of events struck McKenna with another twinge of melancholy. To rehash if-onlies over and over again in her mind did no good. Things were as they were, and neither McKenna, her parents, nor Arrosa could change them.

McKenna refused to allow Mother to sleep on the floor, despite her mother's insistence. When she was a young girl, she'd been corrected a time or two for her tenacity and determined behavior. But now, as an adult, it served her well. Mother acquiesced, and McKenna huddled on the floor on the only remaining thin blanket.

Someone playing what sounded like a tuba in another apartment, the sound of motorcars outside the window, and other undistinguishable commotion kept McKenna from sleeping. Thankfully, both Mother and Arrosa slept soundly despite the ruckus. McKenna wandered to the window. Below, two men shouted at each other, and one of them hit the side of the building with what appeared to be a bat. Another man, in a drunken stupor, staggered down the broken sidewalk. A mangy dog cowered in the corner, and one of the men pushed the other.

In Hollow Creek, things could become disorderly given the saloon not far from the boutique; however, McKenna had never seen such disturbance as what she witnessed below. Was it even safe for Mother and Arrosa to remain here?

When the creditors converged on their home like vultures, Mother contacted her family members, including Aunt Julia Mathilda, their brother, and a distant cousin in Omaha. No one would help, except for Aunt Julia Mathilda who offered McKenna a job at the new shop in Hollow Creek—with numerous stipulations, of course.

Father also attempted to contact his only living family—an uncle and aunt in Chicago, to no avail.

Those who had been friends for years were suddenly foes. They turned their noses up at McKenna's family, whispered behind their backs—and even amongst themselves at times directly in front of the Chapmans—and acted as though they didn't know them.

The pain was almost too much to bear, especially for Mother, who'd prided herself in having close friendships with those of higher society.

In the blink of an eye, they had gone from being one of the wealthiest families in Missoula with an excellent reputation to being poverty-stricken and, in Father's case, jailbound, and of substandard repute. Beggars in their own city and penniless when they'd once supported nearly every charity.

McKenna returned to her place on the floor. At least in Hollow Creek no one knew of her family's situation. She'd done her best to hide behind a façade of uppity importance. Little good that did her now with her family's suffering.

The following morning, McKenna awoke early to make breakfast for Mother and Arrosa before Mother left for her job and

McKenna visited Aunt Julia Mathilda. There wasn't much food and she hadn't learned to cook but a handful of items, but she scrambled the two remaining eggs and cut from the bread loaf a plain piece for each of them. That would have to do.

It was odd how reminders of things of the past entered one's mind at the most peculiar of times—and for the most peculiar of reasons. Who would have thought McKenna would miss the toast Cook made for them in their new General Electric toaster? She could still taste the creamy butter slathered on the tops.

But lamenting about things that would never again be would do her no good. Nor would it benefit Mother or Arrosa. She squared her shoulders and lifted her chin. It would all be all right. Wouldn't it?

She cut up the piece of bread into small bites for her sister and divided the scant portion of eggs, giving Mother the most as she would need her strength for dusting, mopping, and shaking the rugs—and anything else her employer deemed necessary that the live-in maids didn't already tend to.

"Do you prefer the housecleaning over the laundress position?" she asked Mother. They'd both crowded around Arrosa's bed to eat breakfast, McKenna balancing haphazardly on the broken chair.

"I do. It offers more of a variety and is easier on the skin." Mother had once prided herself in looking more youthful than her fifty years. She'd purchased the best tonics and lotions money could buy. The cleansing cream alone, made from orange flour water and almond oil, was purchased from a drug store on Bexar Street that catered to the affluent. "Do you recall that wonderful-smelling massage cream you two purchased for me last Christmas? I can still recall the scent of cucumber every time I used it."

McKenna remembered clearly that day she and Arrosa boarded the streetcar to find the lotion Mother requested on her gift list. The snow swirling about, the large Christmas tree in the city center, the carolers, and the tasty peppermint hot cocoa from Millie's. Oh, yes, she remembered that day. Arrosa had been healthy with a rosy glow from the cold air as they hooked arms and traversed downtown's numerous shops and boutiques without a care in the world.

She gently squeezed Mother's arm. "Someday, we'll find that wonderful-smelling massage cream for you again."

Tears glistened in Mother's eyes. "Well, of all things in the world, special lotions are not what's important."

But the lotion *was* important to Mother, and someday maybe McKenna would be able to afford it.

"Oh, dear." Mother stood. "The time has plumb gotten away from me. I best be on my way." She kissed the top of Arrosa's head, then McKenna's. "Thank you for breakfast. I shall be home this evening after taking the train to visit with your father." A smile crossed her face. How delightful it will be to see him again."

McKenna watched Mother leave, the unshed tears pooling in her eyes. It was only after the door shut that Arrosa spoke. "Do you ever wonder what might have been?"

"If Father hadn't embezzled?"

"Yes."

McKenna knew there was more to their rapid decline in society than just Father's embezzlement. She assumed the uncontrolled spending contributed as well, especially with the second home, another automobile, and treatments Father paid for that were to have cured Arrosa. "I do think of it from time to time."

"I think of it *all* the time." Arrosa sighed then closed her eyes. "If only I hadn't taken ill."

"You mustn't blame yourself. No one asks to be unwell."

McKenna set the plate on the table and returned to sit next to her sister. "I have missed you, even in my short time in Hollow Creek."

"I've missed you too, and all those glorious times when things were different." Arrosa blinked. "Do you remember Leonard?"

"How could I forget him?"

"Such a cad."

For a moment, McKenna saw Arrosa's eyes light the way they once did when she spoke of something that either bothered or thrilled her. "He was a cad."

"And now poor Mother is working for his parents, among other clients."

"She is?" Why hadn't Mother mentioned it?

"Yes. She cleans their house and does errands."

"That has to be difficult seeing as how she and Leonard's mother were friends."

Arrosa offered a slight nod. "Yes, and while Mother doesn't say as much, I suspect she is not treated with the respect she deserves." As if the long sentence wearied Arrosa, she winced and took several struggling breaths.

"Don't try to talk."

"I just—I just want our lives to be as we planned." She stared at her swollen wrists. "You marrying Leonard and me marrying too and someday having many children."

Arrosa had always wanted a passel full of children. Would she even be able to be a mother now what with the effects of her illness? Would her heart be too weak for her to make it to that day when she found a suiter who loved her? An ache tore at McKenna's throat. All those dreams, all those plans. And now? McKenna's parched tongue cleaved to the roof of her mouth, reminding her she'd not had a sip of anything all morning. She assisted Arrosa with a drink of water, tended to her other needs, then prepared to see Aunt Julia Mathilda.

Surely such an excursion would remove from her mind the melancholy thoughts and sorrow she felt for the sister she loved.

CHAPTER SIX

CLAYTON ASPIRED TO BE just like Pa, who'd had an impeccable reputation. Long known in Cullman County, Montana, as one of the most dedicated and decorated lawmen, there were only two types of folks who didn't appreciate him. One was the criminals he apprehended. The other? A man by the name of Richard Rantz.

Rantz had lost when he ran for sheriff against Pa in Cullman County years ago. After Pa died, another man took the post of sheriff when he was elected over Rantz. And now, in Hollow Creek, Clayton won the election garnering seventy-five percent of the vote against the man.

No wonder he held a grudge.

Why Rantz moved to Hollow Creek was beyond Clayton. He eyed the man standing outside the saloon speaking with one of the business's most frequent customers. Clayton reminded himself he wasn't out here in the early evening to lollygag but to do one of the most undesirable jobs a sheriff must do—clean up the manure in the street.

He looked forward to the day when everyone drove an automobile and there would be fewer horse apples to shovel off the main street.

Clayton flung the shovel over his shoulder and with his other hand, hauled the metal can he'd deposit the manure in before loading it into the wagon and hauling it away. He stopped first at a sizable pile just off the boardwalk in front of the mercantile. Scooping it and dumping it in the can, he worked quickly before moving to his next stop in front of the hardware store.

Fortunately, this was a slow time of day and not many people were out and about. Nothing was worse than partaking in this job when traffic was heavy. He discarded his shovelful into the can when he heard a familiar voice.

"Well, looky here."

He glanced up to see Rantz puffing on a cigar and staring at him. "What do you want, Rantz?"

"Is that any way to speak to a fellow lawman?"

Except you aren't a lawman.

Clayton continued his duty, hoping to finish it efficiently because the list of things for him to do before the sun set was lengthy. He walked a few steps to the right, set his shovel on the ground, and cleaned up more of the manure when he saw Rantz shove over the can.

Manure spilled just as Rantz lifted a foot and kicked the metal can, causing it to roll and deposit more of the horse waste on the ground in a thin line. Clayton forced himself to take a few slow, steady breaths as he prayed the Lord would guard his tongue and quell his temper.

"Oh, sorry about that," said Rantz, taking another puff on his cigar. The smoke swirled in the air in Clayton's direction.

Clayton ignored his nemesis, tilted the can right side up, and once again began scooping the spilled manure.

"Ain't you got nothing to say?"

"Not to the likes of you."

Rantz stomped toward him. "What did you say, boy?"

Clayton lifted his head and peered around him. Two people had noticed the altercation. The drunk from the saloon Rantz was previously talking to and the little boy who sold copies of the newspaper.

"Be on your way, Rantz."

"Just because you supposedly had more votes than me doesn't mean you can tell me what to do," he seethed through gritted yellow teeth.

Lord, keep me from saying what I want to say. Clayton took a deep breath. "I did have more votes. You need to move on."

"Men, is there a problem?"

Clayton turned to see one of the highly-respected local ranchers named Thad Evanson. "No, sir," he answered.

"Good to hear it. And you, Rantz?"

Rantz muttered an expletive under his breath, turned on his heel, and walked away.

If only Pa was still alive. He'd know how to handle the ongoing problem that was a wannabe lawman named Rantz.

Patrolling the county was one of Clayton's favorite parts of his job. It enabled him to check on folks he might otherwise not see in the vast expanse of Hollow Creek County. After aiding a man with a broken wagon wheel, he started on his way back home.

Oddly enough, he couldn't remove the man from his mind. Something about him seemed suspicious, but then it could be that Clayton constantly had to be vigilant. Riding the range offered a different variety of attentiveness than handling matters in town or in the vicinity. He couldn't imagine being a lawman in the city what with all the people.

Perhaps it was the man's eyes that troubled Clayton the most—dark, beady, and wide-spaced. He had a hook nose, a scruffy black mustache, and a spotty goatee in the middle of his chin. Thick bushy eyebrows, ears that stuck out from his face, and a few missing teeth drew Clayton's attention, as did a scar above his right eye.

But folks could be homely, have a voice that didn't match their appearance, and have eyes that darted around and still be law-abiding citizens.

In this man's case, he was in a hurry to get home to his family. Or so he'd said.

Weary from the prolonged ride, Clayton tethered his horse when one of his deputies approached him. "These just arrived from Missoula." Deputy Ivinson handed him a bag with a stack of papers inside.

Wanted posters.

It was time they updated him on the latest criminals, some of which escaped the city and hoped to seek anonymity in the more rural areas. Most of them committed more crimes in an area less cautious and attentive.

Areas like Hollow Creek.

Clayton stood just outside the sheriff's office and flipped through the stack of papers. So far he hadn't seen any of the men and one woman in the latest collection.

Until he reached the second-to-the-last poster. A dark-haired man with beady and wide-spaced eyes and a hook nose stared back at him.

A man named Pietro Salazar.

Clayton stuffed the posters into the bag, flung open the door to the sheriff's office, tossed the bag on his desk, and raced to his horse. If he hurried, perhaps he could still catch Salazar before he disappeared.

Urging his horse as fast as it could safely go, Clayton cut across and took a shortcut to the area where he'd last seen the man. His heart pounded in his chest. If he could have apprehended an outlaw and didn't, he'd never forgive himself.

The sun was setting when he stopped and dismounted. He saw the wagon tracks and the cold coals from where a fire had once been. But no Pietro Salazar.

Rantz was waiting for him when he arrived at the sheriff's office early the next morning. "Heard you let a wanted outlaw escape. Helped him, in fact."

Clayton was not of the mind to deal with Rantz. "Who told you that?"

Rantz shuffled through the stack of papers and slammed his fist on the one with Pietro Salazar's face on it. "It's all over town. You don't have to do any sleuthing to figure that out."

"All over town?"

"Word travels fast. I heard it down at the barbershop."

Clayton inwardly groaned and fisted his hands at his sides. "I didn't realize he was a wanted criminal when I helped him. I was doing what we always do—offer assistance to those who need it."

"Tell that to the widow who lost her husband to Salazar's ruthless ways. Or tell that to the cattle ranchers he's stolen from. Or the women he's assaulted. Or the man over in Cullman he beat within an inch of his life. Tell them about your careless ways. I'm sure they'll appreciate your flimsy excuse." Rantz's eyes narrowed, and a muscle twitched beside his right one. "Could be that you ain't suited for this job."

There were times in life when the temptation to do something was great. Clayton faced that temptation at this very moment. He opened his mouth to say what was on his mind, but with effort, clamped his jaw closed. Rantz hoped to antagonize him. Giving in to that goal would only make matters worse.

Clayton clenched his jaw and prayed the Lord would stay his tongue.

"What? Outta words?"

His annoyance flared. "I've got nothing to say to you, Rantz."

"'Cause you know I'm right." Rantz leaned so close that Clayton could see every wrinkle, every scar, and every imperfection on the man's face. He could smell his foul tobacco breath and could see the small chip on his right upper tooth. "You're an idiot, Beringer. You're incapable of the intelligence and fortitude it takes to be a sheriff. I've said it before, and I'll say it again. I have no idea how you ever got elected."

"And you're a louse." The word escaped in what Clayton would call an on-accident on-purpose moment.

Rantz raised his hand, his index finger within inches of Clayton's face. "Watch your step, boy. It wouldn't take much to relieve you from this position."

"Is that a threat? Against a lawman, no less?"

"You ain't seen a threat."

"I think it's best you leave, Rantz."

Rantz threw back his head and chortled. "Now the young'un here is telling me what to do. I'll stay if I want." His face reddened and a vein pulsed in his forehead. Rantz puffed up his chest, and his expression revealed an unspoken threat. "Tell you what. You are both green and yellow. Green because a man like you with no experience ought not to be keeping the law. And yellow because you're a coward and couldn't capture a criminal even if you were given the chance."

Every one of Clayton's muscles tensed. Rantz's calloused words were like a punch to his gut. He may be young, he may be inexperienced, and he may have made a profound error, but he was not and never would be a coward. Ever. Heat flushed through him. He stood and came face to face with Rantz.

"What? You gonna do something?"

With effort and prayer, Clayton bit back the words he wanted to say. He was a man of God first and foremost and secondarily, the son of Sheriff Lamech Beringer. He'd not taint his father's reputation by placing a well-thrown punch square into Rantz's furry jaw, even if the man deserved it.

"You're not worth it," he muttered and took a seat again behind his desk.

Rantz's eye twitched and he opened his mouth, then promptly shut it. Without another word, he turned on his heel and stomped from the sheriff's office, slamming the door behind him.

"Surprised you let him talk to you that way."

Clayton peered over at his one inmate for the day, a man about his age named Malachi Callahan. "Not much else I could do."

Callahan shrugged. "For what it's worth, I voted for you. Would rather have you for the sheriff than Rantz."

"I'm much obliged for that."

Callahan offered a clipped nod then took his place again on the cot in the corner. The young man had been involved in an altercation last night and would be here until tomorrow when the judge heard his case.

Clayton saw Rantz across the street outside of one of the saloons talking with the mayor, one of the more affluent Hollow Creek individuals. He was pointing at the sheriff's office, and even from where Clayton stood tucked beside the window, he could ascertain that Rantz remained indignant.

He lifted the wanted poster from his desk and read through the details again, the regret causing his stomach to clench. His error put innocent people at risk.

Pa would never have made such a careless mistake.

Pietro Salazar's ugly mug stared back at him. Mangy dark-brown hair, empty eyes, and a full and scruffy beard.

WANTED DEAD OR ALIVE
$1,000 for the capture of Pietro Salazar
Wanted for the murder of several unarmed men, assault, horse thievery, train robbery, and cattle rustling. Do not approach as Salazar is a cold-blooded killer. If seen, do not attempt to approach or apprehend this cold-blooded killer. Contact your local lawman immediately.

Rantz's words echoed in Clayton's mind: *"Tell that to the widow who lost her husband to Salazar's ruthless ways. Or tell that to the cattle ranchers he's stolen from. Or the women he's assaulted. Or the man over in Cullman he beat within an inch of his life. Tell them about your careless ways. I'm sure they'll appreciate your flimsy excuse."*

His excuse was a flimsy one. That he was attempting to help someone he thought was in trouble. That he hadn't known the man in the wagon was a wanted outlaw. Was the wagon even his?

Salazar could have shot him in the back as he rode away. The fact he didn't was God's grace and protection alone. But having missed the fact that the man he assisted on his way was a vile convict caused Clayton to once again doubt his abilities as a sheriff. All he'd ever wanted was to make Pa proud and to convince the folks of Hollow Creek he was the man for the job.

He'd failed on both counts.

Ma lived just outside Cullman in a house Pa and Clayton built years ago. To hear that Salazar had beaten a man nearly to death in the town where his mother resided only reinforced the fact that it was time for Ma to move to Hollow Creek. Perhaps this time she'd listen to him when he attempted to convince her.

But Ma was a strong woman. She was headstrong and independent, which assisted her in persevering after Pa was killed. Raising a twelve-year-old boy on her own hadn't been easy. She'd taken in washing and sewing and sold baked goods, which along with Clayton's jobs, had allowed them to survive.

And now he needed to tell her—no, not tell her—*insist* she leave the home her husband built and move to an entirely new town.

A town where some didn't embrace her son's new role as lawkeeper.

He tethered his horse to the fence and noticed Ma's three crates of food from the garden she would deliver to the less fortunate. Ma might be headstrong, but she was also the most kind and caring woman he'd ever met. She hadn't much herself, but as she was fond of saying, *"Some folks have far less."*

"Ma?"

"Clayton?"

She rushed through the door and wrapped her arms around him. "I've missed you." She took a step back. "Let me get a good look at you." She regarded him before adding, "Are you getting enough to eat?"

"Yes, Ma. I eat more than my fair share."

"Good. Well, I was just going back to the garden to see if anything else was ready to be harvested yet. Care for some lemonade?"

He'd never turn down a glass of lemonade. Ma didn't wait for his answer but led him into the house where she poured two generous cups of her famous concoction. Famous because it had more sugar than most lemonades. They took their seats on the porch.

"I'm glad you stopped by. I've been needing to talk to you."

"Oh?"

"But first things first. How have you been? How is Hollow Creek?"

"Fine."

Ma stopped rocking and angled her head. "That does not sound like a very convincing 'fine.'"

"I had an incident yesterday is all."

"Tell me about it."

When Pa was alive and he'd come home after a challenging day of apprehending criminals, he'd share about his day with Ma. What he could share, anyhow. Knowing what Clayton knew now, Pa had to keep an awful lot to himself. Otherwise, Ma would have demanded he find a less dangerous profession.

"I didn't realize a man I stopped to help outside of town was a wanted criminal."

"Oh."

Her one simple word held neither condemnation nor judgment but rather invited him to continue, which he did. "I didn't realize it until I returned to the office and one of my deputies delivered a stack of new wanted posters from Missoula. The man, whom I helped, was included in those posters."

"What was he wanted for?"

"Horse thievery, train robbery, and the like."

"Sounds like a pleasant individual."

Clayton chuckled. "Well, because of me, he's still free."

Ma patted him on his upper arm. "You couldn't have known."

"I still blame myself. Doesn't help that Rantz wasted no time sharing his thoughts on the matter with me." Clayton took a drink of his lemonade and allowed the soothing coolness to refresh him.

"I'm sorry, son. Rantz is clearly jealous because he didn't win the position for sheriff of Hollow Creek County. He was an unpleasant sort even when your father was alive."

"He's likely still holding a grudge from the time Pa beat him in the election."

Ma nodded. "Likely so. And then you beat him when he moved to Hollow Creek County and ran there."

Clayton gazed out over the ranchland and in the direction of the Bitterroot Mountains. Cullman County was far smaller than the growing Hollow Creek County. Pa had served the area well during his tenure. Until he lost his life.

"I'm sorry about Rantz and the outlaw."

"Thank you, Ma. I appreciate that." He removed his hat and set it on the table beside his rocking chair. "Pa wouldn't have made this error."

"While your father was one of the most competent lawmen, he made his share of mistakes as well. There were times bandits escaped and times when things went awry. No one is perfect. We pray for God's direction and do the best we can."

"But I want him to be proud." His throat tightened.

"Oh, son, your father was proud of you and if he were here, he'd be so pleased with the man you have become."

"All my life I've wanted to be just like him."

"And you are." Ma stood and wrapped an arm around his shoulders. "You are very much like him. You'll never be perfect, however, and neither was he. But Hollow Creek couldn't ask for a better, more dedicated man to protect the town and the entire county."

Her words assuaged some of his guilt. "Thank you, Ma."

They sat for a few minutes rocking in their chairs and each drinking a second glass of lemonade. He needed to say something else to Ma, but he wasn't sure how she'd respond. Clayton had prayed she would be amenable to his suggestion, but he also knew how content she was. He cleared his throat. "That brings me to my next topic."

Ma refilled their glasses. "Yes?"

"The criminal could be here in Cullman." He threaded his fingers through his blond hair. "Ma, I'd like you to move to Hollow Creek. No sense in you being out here all alone."

"I won't be moving, son."

"But what if I insist? Pa always told me to watch over you if something were to happen to him. I take that role seriously."

"And you've done a remarkable job of it. Your pa would be proud."

More than anything, Clayton hoped it would please Pa the way he cared for his mother, lived his life, and fought for justice. The error in judgment regarding Pietro Salazar clouded his mind, and with difficulty, he pushed it aside. "If there had been a position here, I'd have taken it. Even though Hollow Creek isn't far, it's too far should you need me in a pinch."

"Clayton..."

"If you don't want to move to Hollow Creek, you could move to Missoula closer to Uncle Art. I'd feel better if it was Hollow Creek, and that's my first choice, but Missoula will do if that suits you. There are all types of modern amenities there, and you'd enjoy the botanical gardens, the plays at the theater, and riding the streetcar."

Twin creases marred Ma's forehead. "Do I look like a city woman to you?"

He chuckled at her dismay. "No, you don't. But you might like the city if you gave it a chance."

"Doubtful."

He understood. He wouldn't much cotton to the city either. "Would you at least think about it?"

"Unfortunately, no. You are the best son a mother could have, Clayton, and I love you for it. But I can't move. Especially now."

He attempted to catch her eye, but she avoided it and stared instead at the railing. A railing he needed to repair before returning to Hollow Creek. "Why?"

She released a sharp exhale. "I've been needing to discuss a matter with you for a while now."

"Are you ill?" The thought of losing her too roiled his stomach.

"No, I'm fine. Healthy as they come."

"Then why?"

Ma ceased rocking and faced him. "Do you remember Hal?"

"Yes. We've known him for years."

"We have. And he's become..."

Clayton didn't want to hear what he presumed she would say. He shook his head, and Ma gripped his forearm. "I have dreaded speaking with you about this. I've prayed daily for the words to say and the wisdom with which to say it."

Ma was a beautiful woman—always had been. Pa told her so on numerous occasions. "Hal is a friend."

"He is. And as you know, he was your father's best friend. He was there for us when we needed him, and has still been here for me all these years later." Her breath hitched. "I loved your pa more than I ever thought it possible to love a man. He was my world, my one true love."

"Then why would you even consider Hal?"

"No one will ever take the place of your father. But I do believe I have enough love in my heart for Hal as well."

Clayton set his glass on the table. "So do you love Hal?"

"I do. He has asked me to marry him. We would rent out his house, but he would continue to ranch both his land and mine. He's a good man, Clayton."

"Good man or not, he's not my pa."

"And he would never ask to be. But he does care about you and you've long thought of him as an uncle."

Clayton couldn't deny her words. Hal had never married and had no other family, so he'd visited often and partook in supper many a time. If Clayton was honest, he would credit Hal with them being able to keep the ranch after the year the severe blizzards took the lives of so many of their cattle. After that significantly slimmed the herd, Clayton took other odd jobs working for Hal and other ranchers. There wasn't a way for a young boy and his mother to run a sizable ranch and no way to pay a hired hand anyhow. It had been a struggle at times for Pa working as both a sheriff and as a rancher.

"I don't know, Ma."

"He's a godly man and has been an elder several times at our church. He is kind, generous, and well thought of."

Ma had a point, but Clayton struggled nonetheless.

"I know what you're thinking, son. You don't want someone to take the place of your father, and he won't. He can't replace the husband your pa was to me, and he can't replace the father your pa was to you. But I would like your blessing."

There were few things he could deny his mother, and this was almost one of those times. He would give her his blessing to marry Hal, but that didn't mean he had to agree with it.

CHAPTER SEVEN

MCKENNA BEMOANED THAT SHE'D forgotten to pack one of her more elegant and expensive shirtwaists and skirts for her visit to her aunt's shop. In her rushed attempt to pack as lightly as possible, it slipped her mind. She pulled on her bland day dress that had seen better days. Perhaps Aunt Julia Mathilda would be so busy with her customers she wouldn't notice her niece dressing rather plainly today.

She brushed her hair and fashioned it into the best coiffure she could manage. She held the miniature mirror Mother kept on the overturned barrel that served as an extra table and peered into it. A tired woman with dark circles beneath her eyes and a weary countenance stared back at her. What happened to the glamorous woman she once was?

McKenna smoothed the wrinkles from her day dress caused by being folded for far too long and hastily packed into her carpetbag. Her appearance would have to do.

Thankfully, her ankle felt much better today as she ventured from the apartment. Last night's rain caused mud puddles in the street, and McKenna did her best to avoid them. She failed miserably at presenting herself as clean and tidy when an automobile drove past quickly and splashed dirty water all over her dress.

She groaned and attempted to remove some of the mud with an efficient swipe. However, her attempts were for naught and only served to smear the sludge even more. McKenna peered back the way she had come, then scanned directly in front of her. She was too far in her walk and closer to Miss Julia Mathilda's Fine Dresses than Thorburn Flats, so she proceeded. Besides, there wasn't time to turn back.

When her family possessed wealth, McKenna herself had a time or two cast a haughty glance at those women who were beneath her station. Ironically, she now was the recipient of such disparaging behavior. In Hollow Creek, no one knew of her family's financial demise and the dresses she wore—even her day dress—were at the same level as or superior to most of what the other women in town wore. She could hold her head high with pride. In Missoula, it was a challenge to not dip her head and cower in embarrassment.

Embarrassment because she no longer wore the finest clothing and shame for what her father had done.

With effort, she lifted her head and looked every passerby in the eye. Even the ones who tossed her a supercilious appraisal.

Obviously, not everyone in Missoula was uppity. There were many, many fine people and even more who were not of high society. But for some reason, as she journeyed to Aunt Julia Mathilda's Fine Dresses, only the haughty ones were out today.

To avoid a large crowd gathered in front of the hardware store, McKenna dipped into the street and right into some mud left behind by the rainstorm. It crusted the sides of her shoes, and she sighed. Hopefully, Aunt Julia Mathilda wouldn't notice.

Her aunt may not notice, but Henrietta, the clerk, certainly did. When McKenna entered the boutique, the saleswoman allowed her gaze to travel from the top of McKenna's head to her mud-encrusted boots. "You can't come in here," she hissed.

A woman inspecting a rack of the latest shirtwaists looked McKenna's way and offered an expression of disdain.

"I need to speak with Aunt Julia Mathilda, please."

Henrietta simultaneously pushed McKenna back out the door while whispering, "Proceed to the back door. I'll open it for you."

The back door? That was only for freight. Attempting to not allow her posture to suffer along with her pride, McKenna traipsed around the side of the building, through another un-avoidable mud puddle, and to the back door. Henrietta held it open for her. "Your aunt is in her office."

"Hello, Aunt Julia Mathilda. I'm here to discuss the items I'll be taking back with me to Hollow Creek."

Her aunt rose from her ornate mahogany desk, set down her fountain pen, and gasped. "Whatever happened to you?"

"First an automobile splashed me, then I inadvertently stepped into some mud attempting to avoid a group of people gathered on the boardwalk, and finally, I was unable to avoid a mud puddle while ambulating to the back door, which Henrietta insisted I use." McKenna attempted to keep her temper from flaring, but to do so was difficult. She'd never much cared for Henrietta, and even less so now.

"Such a tragedy." Her aunt rose. "Well, be that as it may, we can't allow you to be seen at the front of the boutique. What would people say?"

Aunt Julia Mathilda was always concerned about people's opinions. Mother said she was even that way when they were youngsters. "Do you have some dresses you wish for me to take to Hollow Creek?"

"I do. They are already stored in trunks, and I'll have my hired hands deliver them to the depot and load them for you prior to your train leaving. Will that be tomorrow?"

"Yes. The eight o'clock train."

"Good. Are you about to open the store?"

"Yes. I think the boutique will do well." Or at least, McKenna hoped it would.

A woman in an expensive ensemble, a new hat, and a pearl necklace peered through the door into the back area. "Yoo-who? Miss Julia Mathilda?"

McKenna's aunt rushed past her and to the woman. "Yes, I'll be right out, Mrs. Knott."

"No need to bother yourself. We can discuss the matter here." Mrs. Knott reached up and adjusted her perfect Gibson Girl coiffure. She tilted her head toward McKenna and scrunched her nose. "And who might you be? Are you allowing street urchins into the boutique, Julia Mathilda? Of course, you do look slightly familiar."

"I'm McKenna..."

"No, I'm not allowing street urchins into the boutique," interrupted Aunt Julia Mathilda. "This is McKenna Jones, and she was just leaving."

McKenna cast a sidelong glance at her aunt. *McKenna Jones?*

"McKenna Jones. Doesn't ring a bell. I must have thought you were someone else. No matter. It's likely you're not someone I would know anyhow." Mrs. Knott waved her hand in McKenna's direction. "Is she staying long?"

"No, she was about to leave." Aunt Julia sashayed toward Mrs. Knott. "I'm so glad you arrived. I have those exquisite dresses we discussed last week. They arrived yesterday morning from Boston."

"Oh!" Mrs. Knott covered her mouth. "Far be it from me to be impatient, but, well, I was impatiently waiting." She offered a saccharine smile that matched her fake laugh.

"McKenna, I believe we are finished here. If you have any questions, let me know. Otherwise what we've already discussed will occur tomorrow morning at eight o'clock. On with you, now. Please exit from whence you came."

"Yes, ma'am," she mumbled before turning on her heel and leaving the boutique as tears stung her eyes. Her heart constricted. Had her aunt forgotten she spoke to her own niece?

Aunt Julia Mathilda's words tore at her heart. Wasn't family supposed to be loyal? Weren't they supposed to love unconditionally and offer help when times were tough? While Mother mentioned she and her sister were never particularly close the way McKenna and Arrosa were, shouldn't family still care if someone suffered?

Even if a part of that suffering was due to a grievous error on Father's part?

As dejected as she felt, McKenna promised herself she would not return to Mother's apartment until she'd found a way to secure more food for her and Arrosa. Tears burned the back of her throat, but she'd not succumb to pity.

There was a way to get through these trying times. She just had to find it.

And beginning at the church her family had attended for years would be the perfect place to start. Hadn't Father said that God would take care of them and they needed only to trust? She wasn't sure how to commence talking to God or ask Him for anything. Sure, they had said rote prayers in church, but her mind had wandered during those times as it had in most of the church services. Now she wished she'd paid better attention.

The walk to her family's former church was a lengthy one, and her stomach growled in response to the meager food she'd eaten for breakfast. Automobiles zipped past, along with the occasional horse-drawn wagon. She passed a hotel, grocery store, hardware store, brothel, and saloon before entering the main thoroughfare. After a half hour, she spotted the church in the distance. Its gray brick with white trim exterior and tall tower with a clock took her back in time to when things were vastly different. She could almost hear the bell in the tower on those two Sundays a year when she and her family would arrive by chauffeured vehicle. Her father's generous offering when they attended was intended to cover an entire year.

She climbed the eight steps to the wooden double door and swung it open.

Inside, two rows of wooden pews lined the immaculate place of worship. She found the church office just to the left.

A woman's voice answered her knock. "Come in."

"Yes, hello..." the woman's name escaped her.

"Mrs. Metzger."

"Yes, Mrs. Metzger. I'm not sure if you remember me. My name is McKenna Chapman. My family and I attended here as recently as last Christmas."

The woman looked down her long narrow nose at McKenna. Or perhaps she only imagined it due to feeling self-conscious with her mud-covered dress and shoes.

"I vaguely recall your family. Is your father Egbert Chapman?"

"Yes, ma'am." Her voice wavered in her own ears.

"The one who embezzled from the bank?"

McKenna stared down at the floor. Mrs. Metzger wasn't the only one who had referred to Father that way. "Yes, ma'am."

"What is it you need?"

"Might I inquire as to help for an indigent family?"

Mrs. Metzger drummed her fingers on the desk. "You'll have to ask Reverend Metzger about that. He should be in the sanctuary replacing the candles." She gave a dismissive wave of her hand

"Thank you." McKenna left the office and wandered through the sanctuary. She spied the reverend near the pulpit. "Sir, may I speak with you a moment?"

"How can I help you?"

"I'm McKenna Chapman. My family attended here."

Reverend Metzger nodded. "Yes, I recall. Isn't your father the one embezzled from the bank?"

"Yes, sir. I was wondering if the church would be willing to assist a destitute family."

"What family is that?"

"My family." She choked the words, then prepared herself for his response.

"Your family? Hmm. I see." The reverend rubbed his chin. "Unfortunately, we've spent our allotted charity amount for this month. Perhaps you could come back at the beginning of next month."

Could he see the dismay written on her face? "Oh. All right. Thank you."

Father would be the first to admit his wrongdoing, and he had. He'd offered a guilty plea, much to his lawyer's disturbance. But Father knew he'd made a grave mistake when he felt there was no other way to pay their mounting debt. And then add in the sham of a healing retreat he paid thousands of dollars for in the hopes of securing healing for Arrosa.

McKenna trudged down the street. Passersby strolled by, unknowing that a family struggled to survive. That a young woman lay sick in bed. The aroma of turkey and fresh bread filled the air as she passed by the Bellerose Restaurant. She inhaled the glorious scent while her stomach simultaneously grumbled. It reminded her of Thanksgiving when Cook would bake a glorious feast that included extra pumpkin pie.

She came upon a brown-brick church with a tall steeple. Numerous people were outside in what appeared to be a food sale of some sort. Several tables with baked goods, eggs, and other food items lined the sidewalk. Folks milled about and talked.

McKenna stopped by a table with cakes, pies, and cookies. Her stomach rumbled again. But she wasn't here for the decadent desserts. She was here to humble herself once again and inquire whether this church might help Mother and Arrosa.

"My wife made those, and I daresay they are delicious." An older man with kind gray eyes rubbed his stomach. "I ate far too many last night." He chuckled. "She was surprised I left any to sell."

McKenna offered a half smile at the man's comment. "Yes, they do look appetizing."

"Would you care to purchase one? We're raising funds to support our missionaries."

If only she had the funds. But McKenna had only enough for her train fare for her return trip to Hollow Creek. "My apologies, but I won't be able to purchase any desserts today. However, I was wondering if you might know where I could find the pastor of this church?" The words tumbled from her mouth in a rush.

"I'm the pastor of this church." The man extended a hand. "Pastor Shay."

McKenna shook his hand. Should she—could she—ask for charity once again with the very real possibility of being rejected twice in one day? The memory of Mother's chapped and peeling hands and Arrosa's swollen wrist and ankle joints and worsening rash confirmed her decision.

She would do whatever it took to help her family.

76

"It's a pleasure to meet you, Pastor. Might I inquire as to whether your church assists destitute families?"

"We absolutely do. Who do I have the pleasure of meeting?"

McKenna dawdled a bit before sharing her name. Should she offer a false surname as Aunt Julia Mathilda had to the woman in the boutique? But that would be lying, and lying to a clergyman was even worse than telling a falsehood to just anyone. If she did share her name, would Pastor Shay turn her away because he, too, had heard one of the biggest stories of the year in Missoula about a man who robbed a bank of countless dollars through a bookkeeping scheme?

She slowly lifted her head and peered into his expectant face. "I'm McKenna Chapman."

"Nice to meet you, Miss Chapman. Now tell me, how can I assist the destitute family of whom you spoke?"

There was no recognition on Pastor Shay's face, and McKenna released the breath she'd been holding.

"It's my mother and my sister. My sister is quite ill with rheumatic fever."

Pastor Shay's brow furrowed. "I'm sorry to hear that. Why don't I find someone to tend to this table, and you can follow me into the church? I'll take the name and address of your family, and we'll deliver some food items."

McKenna bit her lip as emotion surged to the forefront. The church would help? Even the family of a criminal? "Yes—yes, sir. Thank—thank you."

Humility was an interesting thing. McKenna would be the first to admit she'd been a prideful sort with nary a want in the world. But as of late, she'd had to toss her vanity aside and cease putting on airs—at least in Missoula. She followed Pastor Shay inside the church where several women were preparing more goodies in the foyer.

He grabbed a pencil and paper. "I assume the last name is Chapman?"

"Yes."

"And the address?"

"Thorburn Flats, Apartment 12. Are you familiar with the area?"

"I am. We have served others in that vicinity."

Pastor Shay wrote down the information. "You mentioned your sister is ill. Is there any particular food item that might be the most helpful for her?"

Arrosa loved blueberries. In the day of plenty, her sister would partake in the fruit until she had a stomachache. But could one find the food in Missoula at this time of year for a reasonable price? She didn't want to cause financial hardship for the church. McKenna debated for several seconds before finally saying, "My sister does love blueberries."

"Ah, a good choice indeed." Pastor Shay wrote the word on the paper. "And are they in need of anything else? We do have a clothing benefaction where we collect gently used items from our parishioners to donate to those in need."

"Clothing?" She stumbled on the word as memories of fancy and glamorous clothes of the most expensive variety flashed through her mind. A closet full for each of them. New ones each year so as to stay in proper fashion for the society events they regularly partook in. When the creditors took the home, they also took all but a few pieces of clothes apportioned to each family member.

She finally found her voice again. "Yes, Pastor Shay. They do need clothing and bedding if you have it. However, I don't wish to take from the needs of others less fortunate."

"God provides."

The simple statement caught her unaware. If God provided, why were things the way they were?

"I'll see that your family receives food, clothing, and bedding. And for you?"

"Nothing for me. I work in another town and send money home."

"That's gracious of you, but we have a rule here at the church. Those in need don't leave without at least *something*. How about a few loaves of bread and a chocolate cake?"

How could she refuse that? "Thank you so much."

"You're welcome. Now before we finish, two questions. Do you and your family attend church?"

"Would that determine whether my family receives the food and clothing?"

Pastor Shay shook his head. "Not at all."

"Then, no, not regularly. We once attended a church here in Missoula on Easter and Christmas each year." While beforehand she thought that sounded noble, now hearing herself say it, the twice-a-year ritual sounded paltry.

"And one last question. Can I pray with you before you go?"

"Pray with me?" No one had ever offered to pray *with* her. The routine prayers they'd prayed at church were the only ones she'd ever heard. "I suppose so, yes."

Pastor Shay bowed his head and folded his hands, and McKenna imitated him. "Dear Heavenly Father, we are so grateful for Your providence. But more than that, we are grateful for the sacrifice of Your Son on the Cross. Thank You for giving us eternal life through Him. Please help McKenna's family, and we pray in particular for her sister. Please heal her fully and assist those who care for her in her time of illness. In Jesus' Name, Amen."

McKenna wanted to ask how the pastor could feel so comfortable speaking to God that way. Did He even hear the words? But of course, He would hear the prayers of a clergyman.

After receiving the loaves of bread and chocolate cake, she gratefully bid Pastor Shay goodbye. And as she walked to Thorburn Flats, Father's words re-emerged in her mind. *"God will take care of us. We only need to trust."*

But how could she trust Someone she didn't even know?

Much crowded her mind. First, how she may have solved the problem of Mother and Arrosa's poverty. While only temporary and the church could only offer so much, it was a start. Hopefully, combined with McKenna's continued pay and Mother's earnings from housecleaning, they would be able to survive.

McKenna would just need to sell an abundance of dresses, hats, and jewelry. She'd already presented herself as someone with airs and she had no doubt she could successfully interact with those of high society. Such wasn't outside of the realm of possibility since she herself had once been part of that culture. The irony of the difference between how she presented herself in Hollow Creek and how she really was in Missoula didn't escape her attention.

Her thoughts turned to Mother. Had she arrived yet in Bleakney? If so, how was her meeting with Father? If only McKenna earned enough to send Mother to see him each week.

Shuffling the bread loaves and cake in her arms, McKenna rounded the final corner and onto Thorburn Street. If Pastor Shay was able to find some blueberries for Arrosa, it would mean everything to her. If not, at least there was fresh bread and chocolate cake. With effort, she managed to turn the doorknob of the main door to the apartments and shove it open with a kick of her foot. She bumped it closed with her hip and ascended the stairs.

Once inside, she set the food on the table and checked on Arrosa. Her sister stirred before opening her eyes. "McKenna?"

"I have a surprise for you." She'd not tell her sister about the blueberries just in case that didn't come to fruition.

"A surprise?" Arrosa's sullen eyes lit. "You know how I like surprises."

"Indeed. And I also know how you relish chocolate cake."

Arrosa licked her lips. "Do I ever! Do you recall when Cook would make the most delicious cakes? When Mother was out and doing her charity work, Cook would cut us an extra-large slice. I can taste it even now."

"Oh, yes. And that was a secret that we kept just between the three of us."

"I wonder where Cook is now?"

"Likely spoiling other children with her gift of baking." McKenna patted her sister on the arm. "I'll be right back with a slice for each of us."

She returned a few minutes later, propped Arrosa up on pillows, plopped in the chair with the four good legs, and fed Arrosa the decadent cake.

"Do you remember that time we went to the Christmas ball, and Leonard asked you to dance about fourteen times?"

"Oh, yes. I remember." How could McKenna forget Leonard? He returned to her thoughts from time to time although less and less frequently these days. The man was charming, handsome, witty, wealthy, and owned a brand-new Studebaker. But after Father was accused of embezzling, Leonard promptly disappeared after a yearlong courtship.

"I'm sorry, I shouldn't have reminded you about him." Tears glistened in Arrosa's eyes. "I was just recalling how the other young men hoped to dance with you, but Leonard wasn't so obliging and filled your dance card with every dance from the waltzes to the polkas, and even the grand march. It's awful how he decided to break off your courtship because of what happened."

"Not to worry. I rarely think of him these days. It was heartbreaking at the time, and I remember wondering how I would ever recover from his disloyalty, especially given that a woman of twenty-four is well on her way into spinsterhood. Even in the twentieth century." McKenna thought of how the devastating news of Leonard's decision further compounded all that had transpired. "If I ever fall in love again, I won't place importance on the things that I once found essential for a future husband."

Arrosa mustered a half smile. "What traits would you find of importance now?"

"Witty, of course, and hopefully handsome, but I would look for someone who is loyal, kind, dedicated to his family, and hardworking."

"I would look for those things too. Although I fear a possibility of a suiter for me is unattainable."

McKenna reached for her sister's hand, mindful of her red and swollen wrist. "Someday you will heal, Arrosa, and this will be behind us."

"The doctor visits weekly but says there's nothing to be done but to wait. Sometimes I get so tired of waiting. I want to enjoy life again. I want to be able to help Mother support us rather than fritter away the time by reclining all day." The tears returned.

If only there was a way for her sister to be completely healed, Mother to not have to work so hard, and for Father to be released from jail.

Pastor Shay said that God provided. Would He provide a way through this daunting time?

Early the next morning, McKenna bid Mother and Arrosa farewell, packed her meager belongings in her carpetbag, and proceeded to the train station. True to Aunt Julia Mathilda's word, three enormous trunks were stored on the train at her aunt's expense. She didn't have to ask—she just knew—that she was expected to sell all the clothes, hats, and jewelry contained within them.

Thankfully, McKenna could seek help to load the empty trunks on the train in Hollow Creek to ship them back and the charges would be added to her aunt's account.

Chapter Eight

CLAYTON JUST FINISHED KEEPING the peace between two men who argued nearly every day when he saw Miss Chapman disembark from the train.

Grunting and groaning, two train workers unloaded three oversized trunks and set them next to her on the boardwalk. Had the woman returned to wherever it was she formerly lived to retrieve more personal items? He shook his head. No one he'd ever known had enough belongings—especially clothes—that they needed three trunks. And how did she figure on delivering those to her apartment above Miss Julia Mathilda's Fine Dresses?

He leaned against the corner of the building. McKenna Chapman was an interesting sort. Beautiful with her pale blonde hair and expressive blue eyes. Not that he cared much about dress shops or folks from the city, but there was something about Miss Chapman that intrigued him, even if she was given to snobbery and irritated him in a way he couldn't describe.

Rantz swaggered toward her, and Clayton's protective nature took hold. He pushed off the side of the wall and strolled in their direction.

"I can deliver them for you for five dollars," Rantz was saying.

Rantz had a way of invading a person's personal area, and as he leaned toward Miss Chapman, she leaned away. He continued

84

to sidle up closer to her, and Clayton could clearly hear the words between them.

"You'll do well to take me up on my offer." This from Rantz.

"I'm quite all right, but thank you anyhow." Her voice wavered. Leave it to Rantz to cause her discomfort.

"Miss Chapman, is there a problem here?"

Rantz spun to face him. He squared his shoulders and a muscle in his jaw bunched. "No one asked you, Beringer."

"Didn't say anyone asked me. Miss Chapman, is there a problem here?" Was it his imagination or was the woman relieved to see him?

Likely his imagination. She liked him about as much as he liked her.

"Thank you for your concern, Sheriff. I was just reiterating to..."

"Rantz. Name is Rantz," the man growled.

"Yes, Mr. Rantz, that I did not need his help in transporting my trunks."

Clayton could almost see the flames of anger shooting through Rantz. The man narrowed his eyes. "Was just trying to help is all." He practically spit the words at Clayton.

"Your offer is appreciated, but the woman declined it."

Rantz's face reddened and he ground his jaw. "You need to keep your nose out of things that don't pertain to you, Beringer."

"Ensuring women aren't being accosted by scoundrels is my job. Move on, Rantz. I'll take it from here."

Rantz took two steps closer to Clayton until they were nose to nose. "One of these days, boy, you're gonna get your due," he muttered, cursing under his breath in a tone low enough that only Clayton could hear.

Clayton wanted to tell him he was sick of his threats. Tired of the way he'd harassed two generations of sheriffs. Annoyed with his constant spewing of nonsense from his ill-tempered, uncouth mouth. But instead, he said nothing, just maintained the strong eye contact directed at his adversary.

Finally, Rantz backed up slowly and strode away.

Miss Chapman remained standing by her trunks, clutching a carpetbag. Her mind seemed elsewhere, oblivious to the commotion around her from passersby, automobiles, horses and wagons, and the interaction between Clayton and Rantz.

"Do you need help with the trunks?" he asked.

"I do."

"That's an awful lot of clothes. You didn't steal them, did you?"

She arched a dark blonde eyebrow at him, and he did his best not to smirk. Dare he think she was pretty when she was annoyed? "I'll have you know I never was a criminal to begin with. It was your error in believing I was robbing my own shop."

This time he did laugh. Her serious demeanor exuded calm now that Rantz was gone. Although something told him that Miss Chapman was anything but calm. From what he'd seen, she was an easily riled woman. Or maybe that was just his ability to irritate her.

"I can help you. Let me fetch a wagon, and we'll deliver them to your shop."

"There's just one problem."

"Yes?"

"I will need them delivered to the apartment above the shop. I regret there isn't sufficient room in the shop to store them."

"The apartment above the shop?"

"Yes, please."

He leaned over and grasped the handle of one of the trunks. The thing was heavy. No, not heavy, but weighty as if it contained the entire wardrobe of all the folks in Hollow Creek.

"What do you have in there?"

"Is it too heavy?" The glint in her eye told him there was a modicum of teasing in her glance.

"Too heavy? Nah." He'd never let anyone, especially not a woman, know he wasn't strong enough to do just about anything. He rubbed the back of his neck. Although, his pride wasn't worth a back injury or a hernia.

She set the carpetbag in front of her and propped her hands on her hips. "I never realized clothing and the like could be cumbersome, but if you're unable to help, I understand."

"Unable to help? Who said I'm unable to help? A sheriff does his best to serve the community. You, Miss Chapman, are now part of the community."

He thought he saw a slip of a smile. "I wouldn't want anyone to be injured on my account."

"No one will be injured." Except maybe him. He envisioned himself crouched over, holding his back, all the while in pursuit of an outlaw. He was strong, muscular, and sturdy. Robust from all those years of working on his parents' ranch. However...hauling the trunks down the road or loading them into the back of a wagon was one thing. Lugging them up a steep flight of narrow stairs and through a doorway that didn't allow for anyone tall to enter was entirely a different matter.

He straightened and squared his shoulders. "I'll need to load them into a wagon first to save time. No sense in returning here three times when I could get it handled all in one fell swoop."

"Well, I appreciate it."

He regarded her for a moment. While she was an annoyance, he wouldn't allow her to see him struggle with a bunch of measly trunks. After all, he was anything but puny.

"I'm going to fetch one of my deputies. Because I have a list of things to tend to today, it'll be quicker to have two men instead of one."

Another half-smile lit her face. If the woman was pretty when she frowned, what must she look like with a full smile?

What a dolt. He didn't have time to stand here and ponder a woman's facial expressions. Duties at the sheriff's office were calling him. "Wait here with your trunks. I'll be right back."

Clayton strutted to the sheriff's office, hoping Wiley was still there. Sure enough, his best friend and deputy was sitting in his chair, feet propped on the desk, reading a book.

"Wiley?"

Wiley hid the book behind his back. "Hey there, Clayton. Was just wondering when you'd be back."

"What are you reading?"

"Reading?

"Yes. I saw the book."

"Oh, that. Yes, well, you know me. I do love to read."

"Reading is good, but you're supposed to be working."

Wiley's brown eyes darted around. "I am."

Clayton shook his head. "I need help loading a few trunks into a wagon and carrying them up to the apartment above that new dress shop."

Wiley squinted. "How heavy of trunks?"

"Not too heavy." That was a bald-faced lie.

"Sure. I'll help." Wiley removed his skinny legs from the desk and stood.

They fetched a wagon and returned to the train depot. "Ah, I see why you want to help," said Wiley, who didn't know how to whisper.

"Why?"

"It's that Chapman woman. I think you fancy her."

"Not at all. She's the exact definition of snobbery."

Wiley cocked his head to one side. "You're a terrible liar."

Clayton might as well have been hoisting the trunks by his lonesome. Wiley, while boasting lean muscle, lacked strength. Perhaps he should find a third person.

"Would you prefer to ride in the wagon or walk?" he asked Miss Chapman.

"I'll ride."

He assisted her, and she took a seat on the buckboard. Wiley hopped in back, and Clayton took hold of the reins and steered the wagon the four blocks to Miss Julia Mathilda's Fine Dresses.

McKenna bounced along the rutted road to the back of the shop. While Sheriff Beringer was an irritating sort, she was grateful he'd come along when he had. The man known as Rantz rattled her. There was something about the hateful glint in his eyes that spelled pure evil.

Some women who'd been prattling on in the mercantile before she'd journeyed to Missoula mentioned that Rantz attempted to secure the vote for sheriff of Hollow Creek County. McKenna inadvertently shivered. The man was no more a sheriff than she was wealthy.

Sheriff Beringer introduced the man with him as Deputy Toolin. The slight-framed man with dark hair, a pronounced widow's peak, and a permanent smile seemed the jolly sort and not at all what she would imagine to be a lawman.

But appearances could be deceiving.

She thought of her own self and how she'd once been among the upper-crust community in Missoula. When she'd gone to visit, no one would know she'd previously never baked, cooked, cleaned, scrubbed, or delivered herself anywhere without a chauffeur. The common dress she wore in Missoula yesterday was the farthest thing from the dresses she'd worn when at her previous station in life.

McKenna folded her hands in her lap. Now the dresses she would wear again in Hollow Creek beginning tomorrow would hide her true identity once more. Fortunately for her, Aunt Julia Mathilda refused to allow her to wear anything but the finest of clothing options—which she provided—while clerking at the shop. Anything less would be an embarrassment.

But that didn't mean she had a penny to her name.

The sheriff assisted her from the wagon, his strong and calloused hand gripping hers. She caught a whiff of his after-shaving cream and inhaled. Woodsy and masculine, just as he was. So utterly opposite from the men she'd known in Missoula, including Leonard.

She jolted herself back to reality. Why on earth was she pondering Sheriff Beringer's calloused hands or his after-shaving cream? Must be the stress of visiting Missoula had taken a toll on her.

Should she go inside the apartment? Do anything but awkwardly stand by as the men attempted to unload the heavy trunks? Anticipation zipped through her at the thought of unpacking the trunks and perusing the lovely items Aunt Julia Mathilda had stacked inside.

Not many folks were in the rear of the shop as most preferred the front of the numerous stores that had cropped up on Hollow Creek's Main Street. McKenna focused on the sheriff and his deputy, awaiting a time when she could ask when she should walk up the stairs, unlock the door, and hold it open.

Sheriff Beringer stood behind the wagon and Deputy Toolin jumped up inside. "Push it this way," said the sheriff as he tugged on the handle.

The blue shirt stretched between the sheriff's broad shoulders, indicating the well-developed muscles beneath. Leonard would not have been considered muscular. Nor was Deputy Toolin, who was huffing and puffing and on his knees pushing the first trunk. Should she perhaps see if anyone else could help?

She chastised herself for noticing the differences between the sheriff and Leonard. It was likely there were many more dissimilarities. For one, while the sheriff was utterly vexing, she somehow doubted he would leave someone behind who needed help.

Leonard's dapper face flashed in her mind. He was likely married to someone else now.

She forced her thoughts away from Leonard. She'd never loved him but had only bought into the idea of marrying to secure the wealth of two families. When and if, and it was a big *if* she ever married at this point in her life, it would be for love. Like the love she'd seen between her own parents. A love that lasted no matter the circumstances. No matter the foolish mistake—a mistake with good intentions—that Father had made.

"Don't look now," she heard the sheriff whisper, "but there's Tippi."

"Tippi Harkins?"

"That's the only Tippi I know."

Deputy Toolin panicked. "Can she see me?"

"Yes, unless she's blind."

McKenna turned in the direction the sheriff had nodded. Sure enough, Tippi and her sister, Ophie, were walking down the street. The women had attempted to frequent the shop on that first day McKenna began preparations for the boutique. She'd regrettably had to turn them away, but McKenna found them both to be pleasant.

Deputy Toolin, who had been crouched in the back of the wagon doing his best to shove the second trunk toward the sheriff, now stood, leaving the bulk of the trunk in Sheriff Beringer's arms. He groaned. "Wiley," he hissed.

But Deputy Toolin was standing tall in the back of the wagon and—flexing? Yes, he was flexing his nonexistent arm muscles. "Well, hello, Tippi." He said, his voice deeper than McKenna remembered it being in the few minutes of hearing him speak.

"Ugh, some help here," Sheriff Beringer muttered. Should she help? Attempt to get the deputy's attention?

"Hello, Deputy." Tippi offered a broad smile.

The deputy squared his narrow shoulders and dusted off his shirt sleeves. "Just another day in the life of a lawman," he said, his voice again deepening.

"Oh, yes. Thank you for keeping our town safe," tittered Tippi. Her sister rolled her eyes.

"You're welcome. Of course, we don't only keep the town safe. We also are in the business of serving others. Miss Chapman, for example. When these trunks arrived, the sheriff knew he needed someone strong and capable to assist him with loading and unloading them. He didn't have to look far."

By this time, the sheriff had finally kept the trunk from crashing to the ground and again hoisted it into the back of the wagon. McKenna's eyes met his, and he turned abruptly from her. Was he attempting to hide his reddened face from the effort of ensuring the trunk didn't meet its demise? Or did he fear *he* would meet *his* demise attempting to lift it? Was he hoping she hadn't heard his groaning and grunting after Deputy Toolin left him to balance the trunk on his own?

"Well, we best be off. Good to see you, Deputy. Hello, McKenna. Sheriff."

After the greetings, the women continued on their way.

"You're a dolt, Wiley."

"Not a dolt. Just a besotted man." The deputy lowered his voice. "Did you see her today? If she isn't the most beautiful woman I ever did lay eyes on."

"Never known a man to swoon as much as you do."

"I don't swoon."

"Yes, you do."

McKenna could hold back her amusement no longer as a giggle escaped. It felt good to laugh.

CHAPTER NINE

HE'D NEVER SEEN MISS Chapman offer more than a slight grin. To see her laugh the way she had when he and Wiley had discussed the deputy's apparent affection for Tippi Harkins mesmerized him.

"Clayton? Are we going to finish? I have some reading to catch up on."

He begrudgingly reverted his attention back to Wiley. The guy could be such a jobbernowl. Wiley was the one who'd halted their progress in the first place. "All right. I'm going to pull and you are going to push. On the count of three."

Wiley popped his knuckles, cracked his neck from side to side, then kneeled and pushed with all of his might.

Which wasn't much.

After unloading all three trunks, it was time to attempt to haul them up the narrow, rickety staircase to the apartment. Would the flimsy wood even hold them? That's all Clayton needed—a broken leg. He could see it now, riding his horse and apprehending bandits with one leg hanging there, flopping along outside the stirrup while he rode with haste.

"You probably better go forward, Wiley, and I'll go backwards," he suggested.

"Are you sure? I mean, not that I'm not strong and all, but forward seems better suited for someone like you."

"If I go forward, you'll have to be careful and not trip so the trunk falls on you and crushes you."

Wiley's face said it all. He wouldn't continue to argue.

The first trunk was the heaviest, and Clayton reasoned they should get it over and done with first. He sent Miss Chapman up to unlock the door and hold it open. Clayton crouched and slowly felt for a step before resting his foot on the first stair as he struggled beneath ninety percent of the weight of the trunk. Wiley inadvertently shifted and the trunk rammed into Clayton's chest.

"Sorry about that. You okay?"

"Yes. Let's just get this finished."

Clayton counted the stairs, and on the eighth and final one, which was also the landing, he took a deep breath. Now to get it through the doorway and then on to the second trunk. But he forgot a critical point of concern.

When his head hit the low-hanging doorway, he winced but fortunately was able to maintain his hold on the trunk.

"Are you all right?"

He heard her voice before he saw her and appreciated—but brushed aside—Miss Chapman's concern. "Yes, I'm fine." No sense in her thinking he was a ninny, even though the headache had already started.

They set down the trunk just inside the apartment. Clayton exhaled a deep breath and turned to face Miss Chapman. That's when he noticed the sparse furniture. Only a table and two chairs, a cooking stove, a dry sink, and a potbellied stove were in the main area. A shelf beside the dry sink boasted less than a dozen dishes. He could see through the doorway into the bedroom, and from his vantage point, it too appeared mostly empty.

Why didn't a woman of Miss Chapman's wealth own many possessions? Of course, that was why they were hauling the trunks inside. Perhaps more of her belongings were stored in the unwieldy trunks.

Wiley, meanwhile, had an alternative plan to trek immediately back down the stairs to retrieve the second trunk. He collapsed on the floor, face up, and splayed his arms beside him. "Time for a nap," he said.

If Clayton didn't nudge him outside now, Wiley really *would* take a nap. The man was a hard worker, but he did believe in his daily naps. Even if it meant catching some shut-eye while sitting behind Clayton's desk at the sheriff's office. He teasingly kicked at Wiley's boot. "Get up, Deputy. We have work to do."

"Naw. I'm resting." Wiley peered at him from one squinted eye before shutting it again. He allowed his head to loll to one side and staged an exaggerated snore.

Miss Chapman laughed again, a sweet tinkling sound of joy.

Clayton frowned. This was no time to be thinking of Miss Chapman. The woman was a nuisance, and he needed nothing distracting him from serving the people of Hollow Creek in a way that would have made Pa proud and the citizens grateful they'd elected him last November.

Several minutes later, he and Wiley carried up the second trunk and then the third.

"I really appreciate your help," said Miss Chapman. "Would you like a cup of..." she stalled and scanned her apartment. "Of water? I do apologize, but I have yet to visit the mercantile for provisions since my return to Hollow Creek."

"We're fine, ma'am."

"The sheriff here is going to take me to the restaurant for some grub. I'm starving after all of that hard work."

Clayton jabbed him in the ribs. "We have work to do." To Miss Chapman, he added, "If you need anything else, please let us know."

He hoped his voice sounded as cordial as he intended. Because, after all, if Miss Chapman was still here in Hollow Creek in a few years—which he doubted—she'd be casting her vote for sheriff just like the other citizens.

While she regretted asking Sheriff Beringer and Deputy Toolin to carry the trunks up the stairs to the apartment, it had been a necessity. There was no room in the shop for the cumbersome items, especially since she still had to complete some organizational duties. And by having the trunks upstairs, McKenna could rummage through them at her leisure.

Aunt Julia Mathilda had a gift for cramming as many items as possible inside the trunks. It would be some time before McKenna would require replenishments. Jewelry, magnificent hats, gorgeous shirtwaists and skirts, and numerous pairs of lace-up boots were all stowed in the boxes. She lifted a pair of leather high-heeled black pointy-toed boots from the trunk and slipped her feet into them. Oh, but to have a brand-new pair of shoes once again! She tied the bow midway up and walked through her apartment, sashaying as though she were someone of high society once again.

A normal, more plain pair of boots might cost $2.50, but these, shipped from back East and of the finest quality, sold for $5.25. Nowhere in Hollow Creek or any of the surrounding towns, save for traveling all the way to Missoula, could one find a pair of Ackhurst Lady's Boots.

After traversing around her apartment for a full five minutes, McKenna sat on one of the chairs, removed the shoes, and packed them again inside the trunk. She unfolded a mauve day dress with gold embellishments and large round matching mauve buttons. She slipped it over her head, buttoned it, tugged on some white gloves, and donned one of the four wide-brimmed, fawn-colored hats. A jeweled purse with a chain beckoned her, and she grasped it with her right hand, then again flounced around her apartment. Was it only last year that she owned such attire? All those days of taking her family's wealth for granted. All those times of not worrying about where her next meal or dress would come from.

She swallowed past the unshed tears. Surely someday again life wouldn't be such a struggle. Arrosa would be well, Father would have done his time and would rejoin their family, Mother wouldn't have to work so hard, and McKenna could perhaps own her own boutique rather than be in the employment of Aunt Julia Mathilda.

Until then, McKenna would make the most of the lot life had thrown her. She would continue to work hard and send Mother and Arrosa her wages, all except the meager amount she needed for food and necessities.

She removed the dress, gloves, and hat, and positioned the purse back inside one of the trunks. Aunt Julia Mathilda stored the jewelry in an intriguing wooden box made of matchsticks. Inside, she had arranged exquisite items, including amethyst, turquoise, and pearl necklaces, lockets, and brooches. Such were expensive items for the likes of Hollow Creek, but McKenna had no doubt she'd sell the lot of them to the wealthy ranchers' wives. Her aunt trusted her with such pricey pieces, but McKenna feared she'd lose them or worse yet, they'd be stolen should anyone realize their value. She'd be sure to situate them on a shelf near the rear of the store away from the prying eyes peering in the oversized front window of the shop.

In the heaviest of trunks were two mannequin dress forms and a mannequin head for displaying a necklace.

Tomorrow she would gather some of the items and relocate them downstairs.

And then she'd do her best to sell all of the inventory.

Chapter Ten

EMILIE EVANSON AND HER oldest daughter, five-year-old Adelia, stopped by the boutique a few days later. McKenna brought various items from the apartment and stacked them in the tiny adjacent room that housed a washroom with a separate door and a five-foot-long counter with shelving above it.

"Mrs. Evanson and Adelia, so nice to see you." When Aunt Julia Mathilda offered McKenna a two-week course on how to work at the shop, she'd insisted upon buoyantly greeting each customer who entered the business. *"Even if you must be saccharine or develop a façade, such is necessary if you wish to sell as many items as possible. And I dare say, you must sell as much merchandise as you possibly can."* While there were times McKenna must heed that advice, she genuinely liked many of her customers, especially Mrs. Evanson. The woman was genuine, kind, and gracious. Were it not for her generosity in offering Vera and Morris to chauffer her here from Missoula, McKenna would not have arrived until after the new spur was completed.

"We are in search of something for Vera's birthday. Might you have any suggestions?"

McKenna's favorite task was to unearth just the perfect gift. "I just received some new items." She motioned for Mrs. Evanson and Adelia to follow her to the tiny room. "These handbags are delightful. Might she like one of those? Or perhaps a new hat?"

"I like that one, Mother," said Adelia, pointing to a pink purse with gold embellishments and a brass clasp and chain.

"Oh, yes, this one would do well for Vera. She's been carrying her cumbersome paisley-colored purse for years." Mrs. Evanson twisted the clasp and opened the handbag. "It even has two separate pockets inside."

"That one is truly one of my favorites. It's classy, leather, and functional."

"Might you have something special we could hide in one of the pockets?"

McKenna tapped her chin. "What about this bracelet? I imagine Vera doesn't always wear fine jewelry, but this would be a stylish addition to her Sunday best."

Mrs. Evanson laughed. "Miss Julia Mathilda trained you well, McKenna. Yes, I do agree." She reached for the opal bracelet. "What do you think, Adelia? Would our Vera find this to her liking?"

Adelia smiled and nodded. "Oh, yes. And do you have any cookies we can put in the purse too, Miss Chapman?"

McKenna laughed. Adelia was adorable. If Arrosa were here, she'd offer to assist Adelia in baking a batch of cookies just for Vera. She had a way with children. "Well, I don't sell cookies here, but the mercantile has some delightful candies you could hide inside the handbag with the bracelet."

"Ooh, like a treasure hunt. Can we, Mother?"

Mrs. Evanson planted a kiss on Adelia's head. "I think that's a remarkable idea. Yes, let's tuck all kinds of things inside. Vera will love it." To McKenna, she added, "Do you offer gift-wrapping services?"

"I do."

"Splendid! Adelia and I will visit the mercantile and be back posthaste with more goodies. Vera does have a sweet tooth when it comes to bonbons and taffies. Shall we see if Mrs. Dell has any on hand?"

Adelia bobbed her head. "And some bonbons and taffies for Ephraim and me as well."

"I think that can be arranged. We'll be back momentarily." Mrs. Evanson and Adelia left the store before returning within a half hour with a bag of treats wrapped in tan paper.

McKenna added the price of the purchases, hid the bracelet and candies inside the purse upon Mrs. Evanson's request, and wrapped the purse in elaborate brightly colored paper. She affixed a bow, lace, and a ribbon on top.

Mrs. Evanson handed McKenna the payment. "It's perfect! And so lovely she won't want to open it."

An hour and four customers later, McKenna commenced to finish unpacking the crate of new items from upstairs. She loved her employment at the boutique, even though the unassuming building was far from as dignified as her aunt's store in Missoula. There was no newly installed chandelier, fancy windows, or lush woven carpet. There was no ornately flowered wallpaper on the walls and no tastefully placed flower vases. No expensive glassed-in counters of the finest wood and lavish chairs in which to recline when exhausted from shopping. Instead, it boasted a fresh coat of paint, a swept wooden floor, a dingy counter in need of a good sanding, and a few shelves and makeshift tables for items that didn't fit on the racks or the mannequins. McKenna had, however, taken advantage of the spacious window at the front of the store facing the boardwalk. Two full-sized mannequins, dressed completely in the latest fashions with hats atop their heads, modeled the store's finest wares. Thankfully, the mannequins were not three hundred pounds as some were, as she'd barely been able to drag them to their new location. So deliberate in her concentration of determining which items to set out first, McKenna jolted when she thought she heard the bellpull on the door ring. She stepped out of the back room. "Hello?"

No one answered.

"Hello?" she called again.

Still no answer. She scanned the area but saw no one. McKenna shrugged and returned to her unpacking duties. Just as she unfolded the mauve dress, she heard the bell jingle a second time. She stepped from the room and into the main area when the sight took her by surprise.

A man was shifting between the racks of clothes. She inhaled a sharp breath as her heart raced. Who was this man and why was he in her boutique? Was he dangerous? Did he have ill intent? After all, men did *not* frequent the boutique of their own free will. Unless they were covertly shopping for their wives for Christmas, Valentine's, a wedding anniversary, or a birthday.

The man's frantic gaze caught hers, and he scowled before returning his attention to inadvertently yanking clothes off the racks as he stumbled about. McKenna swiveled her head from side to side. There was no back door to the boutique and only one way out, and that was through the front. Although she could hide.

Wisdom urged her to retreat to the back room and shut the door. Fear kept her rooted in place.

So fearful was she that she couldn't be sure what she saw next was a figment of her imagination or reality.

One of the mannequins from the front window's dark hair jounced as it was carried from its former location. It shielded whoever hid behind her. A someone who looked vaguely familiar.

McKenna held a hand to her heart as her eyes darted about, catching a glimpse of shoulders only—shoulders she presumed to be a man's. The two individuals dodged each other, while one took swings at the other—swings stopped only by the innocent mannequin in the stylish green dress.

The mannequin danced and bobbed about to-and-fro as though a puppet as the one behind it shifted. The fluffy brown wig tottered to one side, exposing a partially bald head.

McKenna feared the arms would snap off, and if that were to happen, her aunt would be most displeased and perhaps even discharge her from her employment. Mannequins were expensive.

She opened her mouth to announce her displeasure when she noticed the man from the clothing racks attempting to leave through the front door.

Good. He had no business here disrupting her store and potentially ruining the expensive dresses.

However, the man did not get far as the other person behind the mannequin turned it sideways, preventing any escape. It was then that she recognized the man holding the mannequin.

Sheriff Beringer.

Such audacity! Certainly, she was in favor of justice and keeping law and order. However, she did *not* approve of using one of the pricey mannequins to do so. Hands fisted on her hips, she stomped in the direction of the commotion.

"You are under arrest, Schultz!" said the sheriff.

The man who'd been formerly rummaging through the clothes and was apparently named Schultz, dropped to his knees, and for a minute, McKenna figured he'd surrender. But such was not the case. Instead, he attempted to crawl beneath the blockade the sheriff had erected using his own self and the sideways mannequin. The dress brushed the floor, no doubt soiling it. McKenna gritted her teeth. If the dress ripped or was otherwise damaged, she would have no way of paying for it.

And Aunt Julia Mathilda would excuse her immediately.

And if Aunt Julia Mathilda excused her immediately, how would she help support Mother and Arrosa?

"I demand you both cease this tomfoolery at once," she squeaked, regretting that her voice sounded the opposite of authoritative.

Sheriff Beringer's eyes widened as their gazes connected. He quickly recovered. "Schultz, you heard the woman. Halt where you are."

"No can do, Sheriff." Schultz again attempted to escape. This time, Sheriff Beringer tossed the mannequin aside and braced himself as Schultz ran toward him. Schultz nearly was able to succeed in getting around him until the sheriff tackled him.

McKenna watched as they scuffled. Round and round they went. Perhaps she could be of assistance. After all, the mere thought of her store being ruined motivated her to take matters into her own hands. She grabbed the broom and stalked to the front of the store. With precise accuracy and swift movements, she whacked Schultz on the back of the head with the straw end of the broom.

"Hey!" He stopped wrestling with the sheriff, bowed his head, and protected it from further blows. "Quit hitting me with the broom, lady."

"How dare you wreak havoc on my store!" She aimed one more time and caught him in the upper arm.

The sheriff stood and gripped Schultz's arm. "You are under arrest."

Schultz's whiny voice emerged amid his attempt to break free from the sheriff's grasp. "Ain't you gonna do something to her for hitting me?"

"Nope."

Schultz growled. "If it wasn't for you, lady, I would be on my way by now."

"I was perfectly capable of apprehending you myself," said Sheriff Beringer.

But Schultz, twice as wide and much taller than the sheriff, attempted to bust past him to no avail. Sheriff Beringer, with his quick reflexes and muscle, as opposed to Schultz's chubby physique, held tightly to the outlaw.

McKenna stepped past the mess and watched from the boardwalk.

The surrounding crowd cheered as Schultz was hauled to the jail. Meanwhile, the boutique was left in disarray with obvious damage to both the mannequin and several of the clothing items haphazardly strewn on the floor.

McKenna stiffened her backbone, pursed her lips, and willed herself not to give in to the emotion surging to the forefront.

Sheriff Beringer would most certainly hear from her about this!

CHAPTER ELEVEN

HE WAS A DUNDERHEAD.

Clayton walked down the boardwalk and to Miss Julia Mathilda's Fine Dresses after locking Schultz up in the jail. Hopefully the man would learn this time that his criminal ventures didn't pay.

He stopped at the front window and peered inside. The store was in complete disarray with clothes strewn everywhere, the mannequin he'd used to block Schultz on the floor with the wig clumped beside it, and several hats—some of them flattened—dispersed throughout. On her knees beside the mannequin was Miss Chapman.

Her shoulders were slumped in a bowed heap. He couldn't tell for sure from this distance, but it appeared she may have been crying.

He needed to rectify this. Posthaste.

Ma taught him to be a gentleman above all else. A woman deserved to be treated in a chivalrous manner, and if that meant humbling himself and aiding her in cleaning up the store no man in his right mind would be seen in, so be it. He cringed when he thought of the mocking Wiley would subject him to if he saw him.

He just wouldn't allow Wiley to see him, and that was that.

Clayton turned the doorknob, but it wouldn't budge. That's when he noticed for the first time that a handwritten *closed* sign hung in the window. Should he knock? Come back later?

No, best to remedy this mess as soon as possible. Better to not delay.

He raised a hand to knock, paused and reconsidered, then finally tapped the windowed door twice.

Miss Chapman shot him a narrow-eyed look before standing and slowly meandering to the door.

It wasn't too late to change his mind.

She opened the door. A superior lift of her chin and the fiery look in her eyes told him she was displeased. But how could she not be?

"Miss Chapman?"

"Yes?"

From this distance, he could see that she had been, in fact, crying. Her blotchy face, red-rimmed eyes, and the handkerchief in her hands were all clues.

"Can I come in for a minute? I promise it won't take long."

She blinked rapidly and took two steps backward, and he thought at first that she would deny his request.

"Yes," she said in a voice so quiet he almost missed it.

He entered the shop and closed the door behind him. No sense in having nosy onlookers interrupt what he needed to say. Or to see him and report it to the town's newspaper reporter, who would write a full-blown article.

"About the...mess."

"Mess?" she asked. "You mean calamity?"

"All right, calamity."

"You had no right to come inside the boutique. I would have gladly ushered the man outside so you could have tended to matters there." Something unrecognizable flickered in her gaze.

A dress, obviously torn, caught his attention, and he inwardly groaned. "I'm sorry, Miss Chapman. At the time, it seemed like the best course."

"And now I'm left to contend with destroyed clothing strewn about as if a tornado whipped through here."

She crossed her arms and waited for him to speak. He searched for the right words to say. "Unfortunately, sometimes crimes are committed in places we don't expect."

The raising of her eyebrows and the way she jerked her head back quickly told him that wasn't the answer she expected.

"I do appreciate your willingness to use a broom on Schultz, although it wasn't necessary."

She pursed her lips.

Clayton rubbed the back of his neck. Truth was, he'd been impressed by her swift actions, and incapacitating Schultz *had* helped him to arrest the man sooner. But he didn't want Miss Chapman to think him inept.

"I think it's best you leave."

"No, wait. Please."

Worry knotted on her brow. "As you can see, I have hours of work ahead of me. Not only that, but I will be losing business as I tend to this unforeseen matter."

While he didn't understand why any woman would want to spend inordinate amounts of hard-earned money on frivolous things like hats and fancy dresses, he knew this was her livelihood. And he'd taken a portion of that away from her. He was not only a dunderhead, but a cad. "I would like to assist you in cleaning up the place."

Indecision weighed in her expression.

"I will also pay for anything that was destroyed."

He meant both promises.

"It will be quite pricey."

"I understand. The county does have a fund for things like this, and what it won't cover, I'll cover personally."

A glimmer shone in her gaze. "Do you promise?"

"I am a man of my word, Miss Chapman."

That seemed to appease her. "I have to keep the shop closed until it's tidied and is in its former condition."

"I understand."

"What about keeping the law?"

He'd already thought of that. "Deputy Toolin is in town for two more days. He's in the sheriff's office right now keeping an eye on Schultz and two other outlaws." *And likely reading.* "It's been a busy morning."

She directed him to a pile of scattered dresses. "You can start with those and then fix the mannequin. I'm attempting to mend a few torn items."

He nodded and proceeded to the pile. A glance back at Miss Chapman reminded him that for whatever reason, he didn't want to disappoint her.

While it surprised her, McKenna was grateful for the sheriff's help. However, being in his presence reminded her of why he was such a vexing individual.

"Why would anyone wear this kind of shoe?" He held up one of the Ackhurst Lady's Boots by the shoelace.

"Begging your pardon, but that shoe is of the latest fashion."

"My ankles hurt just thinking about it." He let the shoe dangle while he scrunched his nose and curled his lip. "You'd have to be out of your mind to wear something like this."

"It's far better than wearing those boots you wear."

He set the lady's boot on the floor and pointed at his own shoe. "What's wrong with these?"

"Besides the fact they're worn, frayed, scuffed, and hideous, not much."

"Hideous? They're functional and far better than some fancy shoe that could cause someone to break her leg."

McKenna tapped her fingers on the counter. "You, sir, obviously have no fashion sense."

He laughed at her comment. "Don't claim to. Men don't need fashion sense. We look for things that we can move in. Not uncomfortable items like this frippery." He held up one of the shirtwaists.

"Frippery?"

"In my way of thinking, one only needs the necessities. Men don't wear things like this. And why spend hard-earned money on frivolous items that aren't only uncomfortable to wear but can only be worn on certain occasions?"

"It's far better than looking unkempt. Appearances are important."

"Do I look unkempt?"

His perplexed expression nearly caused her to regale in laughter. She regarded him. Sheriff Beringer was far from unkempt with his slightly ruffled dark blond hair and his blue flannel shirt and jeans. Truth was, he was rather handsome. But she'd not tell him as much. "Somewhat," she answered. There. Neither a truth nor a falsehood. "Besides, men in the city wear clean, laundered trousers, coats, fedoras, and lace-up shoes, not boots. Therefore, men *can* be stylish as well."

McKenna thought of Leonard. He was stylish with his expensive clothes with nary a piece of lint or a speck of dirt. Handsome, too, with his close-cropped oiled black hair. But he was nowhere near as handsome as the sheriff with his broad shoulders and nice hazel eyes. She bit her lip. Had that thought just entered her mind? And why was she comparing the two men?

The stress of the day had certainly affected her thinking.

"I don't care about fancy trousers, fedoras, or lace-up shoes. I like my shirt, cowboy hat, and comfortable boots and jeans—especially these jeans. They were special-ordered for me from the catalog at the mercantile."

"Hmm. Well, be that as it may, some folks take pride in their appearance. Far be it from me to insist you do the same." She averted her gaze to a skirt on the floor and hastily scooped it up. It wouldn't do for him to see the red that likely crept up her neck and face. For if she were honest, there was nothing wrong with the sheriff's clothing. Nothing that a little laundering and shoe shining couldn't fix. She hung up several more skirts, noting how much they'd accomplished in such little time, and gathered a necklace that, thankfully, hadn't been broken.

If Aunt Julia Mathilda saw the condition of the boutique...McKenna sucked in a deep breath. Her aunt must never know. Especially about the broken mannequin. "I do hope we can fix this," she said, lifting its head.

"I think we can." He stood the mannequin up and began inspecting the fractures from its fall.

"I don't even want to consider how expensive a replacement is." McKenna shivered. It would likely be more than a month or two of her pay to replace it.

He tossed her an inquisitive glance. "Surely with owning a store like this one, you could afford several of these."

"It's my aunt's store, to be exact, and..." she shook her head. "These are pricey."

If he believed her to be wealthy, she had achieved her goal of not allowing anyone in Hollow Creek to know of her family's loss. That modicum of satisfaction was swiftly overshadowed by a niggling reminder that if someone were to find out about Father's embezzlement, there would be no customers at the boutique. Aunt Julia Mathilda even warned as much. That was why McKenna wasn't allowed to work at the store in Missoula. She must ensure Sheriff Beringer didn't discover the truth most of all. A man who prided himself on keeping the law would have no use for anyone who failed to abide by it. Or their daughter.

Not that she cared about the sheriff's opinion. For she didn't. However, if McKenna were to provide for Mother and Arrosa, her secret must be kept at all costs.

She lifted her chin, and her gaze connected with Sheriff Beringer's. He was studying her, and for a moment she feared he could see right through her and know her most secret thoughts.

"I can glue the cracks, and they'll be as good as new," he was saying.

"I'd appreciate that." She'd just do all she could to prevent Aunt Julia Mathilda from ever setting foot in the Hollow Creek shop. McKenna arranged the wig on the mannequin's head. "Much better."

The sheriff chuckled. "I reckon I looked absurd holding this thing while attempting to block Schultz's escape."

"Indeed you did. Fortunately, I didn't notice any passersby at the time."

They both shared a laugh. Oh, but how marvelous it felt given her worries about the condition of the store. "And then," she added, "you turned it sideways and the wig fell off."

He slapped his knee with his hand. "I noticed that. Poor lady."

"Poor lady, indeed!"

Their amusement echoed throughout the boutique. What would someone think if they peered through the window?

When they both sobered, the sheriff spoke. "I truly am sorry for what happened, and I will see to it that you are reimbursed as I mentioned earlier. Just let me know the amount."

"Thank you and I will."

"I also think—if it's all right with you anyhow—that we refer to each other by our given names. I'm Clayton."

"McKenna."

"McKenna," he repeated, and she noted for perhaps the first time the pleasing timbre in his voice.

He held her gaze again, and her stomach fluttered something akin to a bizarre somersault.

They finished tidying the shop before he returned to the sheriff's office. And although she still found him vexing, perhaps it was a little less so.

CHAPTER TWELVE

MCKENNA FINISHED UNLOADING MORE items from the apartment two days later. Thankfully Clayton kept his word and paid for the broken items. McKenna figured it best not to inform Aunt Julia Mathilda about the mishap since all was accounted for.

At noon, the postmaster delivered a letter from Mother. Homesickness filled her heart. Oh, but to have her family here with her! Or to return to Missoula permanently. Her heart yearned for the closeness and comfort her family shared, especially in recent months.

Mother's precise handwriting filled the page.

Dearest McKenna,

I hope this finds you doing well. It was such a delight to visit with you last month. If I haven't yet told you, I am proud of all you are doing in Hollow Creek to help provide for our family.

You will never believe what happened two days after you left. A man by the name of Pastor Shay and his son stopped by for a visit. I had never met the men prior to this day, yet they delivered several crates of food. Preserves, bread, canned goods, fresh vegetables, eggs, milk, coffee, sugar, flour, and the like. They even brought blueberries for Arrosa! I dare say she improved tenfold just from eating those blueberries. They brought some blankets and a dress that will fit Arrosa with minimal alterations.

I truly do believe God is faithful. He sent Pastor Shay and his son with the food at just the time we needed it. Our cupboards and our ice box are full. We now have extra blankets.

Pastor Shay invited me to church on Sunday. I have now attended thrice. When one of the women I clean for discusses the Lord, I am now beginning to understand better that which she speaks of because I have had a desire to read the Bible myself. A desire I never before had.

Your father's trial is scheduled to occur in two months. Pastor Shay says we can bring anything that burdens us to the Lord and He hears us. I have been praying He will allow your father to stay in Bleakney rather than being sent to that horrific prison in Deer Lodge.

Please write and tell me how you fare.

All my love,
Mother

McKenna dabbed at her eyes with a handkerchief. To know her mother and sister had plentiful food warmed her heart. She had profound respect for Pastor Shay. He'd not judged McKenna or her family based on her father's bad decision. If he even knew of that decision.

Instead, the pastor had generously ensured Mother's cupboards and ice box were stocked with food. And the blueberries for Arrosa—what a blessing!

Mother seemed to believe God was faithful. McKenna couldn't be sure as she'd never really known much about the Lord. What if she attended a church here? If for nothing else, she could learn how to pray like Pastor Shay had for her family.

On Sunday, she dressed in her white shirtwaist and blue skirt and walked the short distance to Grace Church, one of the two churches in Hollow Creek. Mr. and Mrs. Evanson, Vera, Morris, and a few women she'd seen in the boutique chatted in their pews before the service started. Mrs. Evanson waved at her and smiled. Was it proper etiquette to request to sit in another's family pew? But from all appearances, the Evansons, their children, Vera and Morris, and another couple took the length of that pew and no other ones in that vicinity were empty.

Suddenly feeling out of place and without a pew of her own, McKenna thought perhaps today wasn't the best day to attend. Then she saw another familiar face.

"McKenna?"

"Sheriff, or rather, Clayton?"

"I didn't realize you attended here."

"It's my first time."

He nodded. "Well, you're welcome to join Wiley and me if you aren't already sitting elsewhere."

Relief flooded her. While the sheriff and his deputy were not her first choices, it was far better than searching for an empty spot beside a stranger, sitting by her lonesome, or leaving altogether. "Thank you," she said, following him to the second-to-the-last pew.

"Hello, Miss Chapman," said Wiley. His hair was slicked away from his face, making his prominent widow's peak even more pronounced. The skinny fellow scooted to the far end of the pew. Clayton gestured for her to slide in next, and he sat on the edge. A flicker of panic zipped through her as nerves overwhelmed her. What if her voice was off-key when they sang hymns? What if what Reverend Arkley spoke of baffled her? After all, she knew so little about the Lord. What if others could tell that she was not a regular church-goer? She gripped her Bible tightly in her hands. Perhaps she shouldn't have come.

But no one seemed to be paying her any mind, with the exception of Clayton, who nodded and smiled. He looked dapper today in his Sunday best, and she diverted her attention from him to Reverend Arkley, who had taken his place in the pulpit. After a few announcements, they sang several hymns, none of which McKenna recognized. When she and her family attended church in Missoula, the congregation sang Christmas songs at the Christmas service, and one or two hymns during the Easter service. Hymns she couldn't recollect.

Surprisingly for such a scrawny fellow, Wiley had a deep singing voice. Clayton's on-tune baritone was pleasing, but as for her own, she feared hers sounded more like high-pitched squawking. McKenna stared at the open hymnal, the words coming alive as she, with effort, kept her volume subdued even as a peculiar fluttering of hope rippled through her.

What a friend we have in Jesus,
All our sins and griefs to bear!
What a privilege to carry
Everything to God in prayer!
Oh, what peace we often forfeit,
Oh, what needless pain we bear,
All because we do not carry
Everything to God in prayer!

Could it be that Jesus truly was a Friend? That she could avoid pain if she'd only offer her concerns to the Lord in prayer? Could Mother be right? That God truly *was* faithful? Could Father be correct when he said God would take care of them and they needed only to trust? Was Pastor Shay truthful when he said that God provided? Were the words of the third verse accurate?

In His arms He'll take and shield thee,
Thou wilt find a solace there.

Or was this just hopeful contemplation on the part of the hymn writer? For how could she take refuge in Jesus' arms since He was in heaven?

They sang two more songs before taking their seats, passing the offering plate, and preparing for the sermon.

"Thank you all for being here today," said Reverend Arkley. While she'd only met him a handful of times, he seemed a kindly and gracious man. "Please turn in your Bibles to Psalm 46. We'll be continuing our sermon series on how the Lord is our refuge."

The Lord was their refuge? And their friend? And He was faithful and could be trusted? And He provided? How had she not known this in all the years of attending the Missoula church?

McKenna opened her Bible, lamenting that the crisp pages stuck together. A quiver of insecurity mixed with anticipation flooded her. With careful effort, she thumbed through the entire book looking for wherever Psalm 46 might be. The smell of ink on the pages oddly comforted her. Perhaps because it reminded her of the days in their elaborate home in Missoula when she would recline in the library with one of Father's many books.

Books that were auctioned away when they'd lost the home.

From her side-eye, she noticed that Clayton found the Psalms quite easily. Perhaps he was a man who spent considerable time in God's Word. From her other eye, she saw that Deputy Toolin was already perusing the verse Reverend Arkley referenced.

Why could she not find it?

What was wrong with her? And what would people think?

She bit her lip in determination. She *would* find the Psalms even if the pages continued to stick together. A tingling swept through her and her stomach pitted into tight coils. She flipped through the entire Book, then back again.

"It's in the middle or thereabouts," whispered Clayton.

When her eye met his, she noticed no condemnation or judgment. Only kindness.

And a different sort of tingling zipped through her from his handsome smile and close proximity.

She nodded, collected her wits about her, closed the Bible, then opened it about midway. Sure enough, the Book of Psalms was exactly where he'd said it would be.

Clayton had attended church since his earliest days. Memories of him, Ma, and Pa sitting on the pew in Cullman flashed through his mind. He missed those days. Missed the way Pa would discuss the sermon on the way home and missed the special apple pie that awaited them every Sunday. Apple pie that was eaten before the noonday meal as part of a tradition his parents invented from the earliest days of their marriage. If only Clayton could go back for just one day and relive those fond memories.

Now Ma was thinking of marrying someone else. She said he wouldn't replace Pa, but Clayton knew he would. How could he not? He'd be the center of Ma's life. Not that Hal *wasn't* a good man. He loved the Lord, obviously loved Ma, and he worked hard.

But he wasn't Pa. Never would be.

With extreme effort, Clayton shoved aside the thoughts and focused on the hymns. Someday, Lord willing, he'd have a family of his own and maybe they could recreate some of the same traditions he had experienced as a young'un.

His attention veered to McKenna. The woman intrigued him. She was uppity, but he reckoned that's how wealthy folks were. Although not all of them. His gaze settled on the Evanson family. Thad and Emilie weren't snobbish, and they were among the most affluent in Hollow Creek.

Clayton could barely hear McKenna's voice as she sang. Was she intimidated? After all, she'd said it was her first time at Grace Church. He cast a glance at her. With her pale blonde hair, expressive light-blue eyes, full lips, and slender figure, McKenna Chapman was a beautiful woman. Before assisting her with tidying the shop, he might have thought her to be more serious with a reserved personality. However, joshing with her about his clothing choices brought a smile to her face. She possessed a charming wit to her words. Her laughter, which he hadn't experienced often, was pleasant to his ears.

But how could someone be pleasant and annoying all at once?

When they finished the final hymn, passed the offertory plate, and took their seats, Reverend Arkley asked them to find Psalm 46 in the Bible. He'd found it easily, but noticed that had not been the case for McKenna. Could it be because of nerves? He shrugged. He'd never take it for granted being raised in a godly family, but he knew that wasn't something everyone experienced. Perhaps that was McKenna's situation. Should he offer assistance? Keep his mouth—which often spoke without his permission—shut? Ignore the fact she was flustered?

"It's in the middle or thereabouts," he finally whispered.

Reverend Arkley's words brought him back to the sermon. The reverend read the words of Psalm 46:1-3, and Clayton followed along in his Bible.

"God is our refuge and strength, a very present help in trouble. Therefore will not we fear, though the earth be removed, and though the mountains be carried into the midst of the sea; Though the waters

thereof roar and be troubled, though the mountains shake with the swelling thereof. Selah.' God is our refuge, our strength, and our help."

The man had a way of explaining God's Word and convicting the heart. There had been times in Clayton's life when he hadn't relied on the Lord. Had put his faith in himself and his abilities rather than Jesus. Or had put someone or something else in the rightful spot only God deserved. He listened intently and was reminded of all the times his Savior protected him while hunting outlaws, chasing bandits, engaging in gunfights, and even working on the ranch back home. Of providing for him and Ma after Pa lost his life while fighting for justice.

McKenna's brow furrowed, and he thought he saw tears hidden in the depths of her eyes. Did she believe God to be her refuge?

Was there more to her than what she allowed folks to see?

CHAPTER THIRTEEN

MCKENNA SET ABOUT HER daily duties at the boutique. All of the items from the apartment had now been combined with the previous goods. Several customers shopped today, and the deposit she'd deliver to the bank this evening upon closing was laudable.

She might just be able to succeed at this endeavor after all.

That evening, she climbed the stairs to her apartment, her feet aching but her heart full. If she continued to sell as much as she had today, perhaps she could request a raise from Aunt Julia Mathilda. A raise would aid Mother and Arrosa. And maybe she could keep aside a smidgen more to purchase a new pair of shoes to replace her worn ones. She ate supper, then sat down at the table by her lonesome. Solitude was not something she embraced, and it left her lonely. She stared out the window at the street below. A drunkard stumbled from the saloon across the street, and in the far distance, she thought she spied Clayton doing his nightly patrols.

If only she had some books to read. If only she could tuck herself away in Father's library and delight in the shelves upon shelves of classic literature. If only she owned even one of those books.

She replaced her garments with her nightgown and plopped on the side of the bed when she spied her Bible on the trunk doubling as a nightstand. There were stories within its pages, and she had nothing else to read. Besides, the Psalm Reverend Arkley discussed in church Sunday remained firmly planted in her mind. Was God only a refuge to those who spent time with Him? Who read His Word? Who went to church every Sunday?

If so, she could do all three of those things and hopefully earn Him as her refuge and not fear what life may toss her way. Not worry about Arrosa succumbing to her illness, Father being sent to Deer Lodge, or Mother's health declining due to her arduous work cleaning houses with little reprieve.

She opened the Bible in the middle as Clayton suggested and again read Psalm 46. She especially liked the last two verses: *"Be still, and know that I am God: I will be exalted among the heathen, I will be exalted in the earth. The Lord of hosts is with us; the God of Jacob is our refuge. Selah."* But what did it mean to be still? To only think of Him? And was it true that the Lord of hosts was with her? Who was Jacob?

An incredible hunger surged through her. Not for bread, fruits, steak, or delectable desserts, but for reading the Book she'd rarely offered more than a passing glance to in the past. Perhaps she could write down all of her questions and ask Reverend Arkley or maybe even Clayton since he seemed to know about the things of God. Or perhaps Emilie Evanson when she next visited the boutique. But in the meantime, since she had little else occupying her time, McKenna would take a gander at the Book that had suddenly and unexpectedly captured her curiosity.

She finally fell asleep at around midnight. It was a peaceful sleep until she thought she heard a noise downstairs in the boutique.

She shot up in bed, heart racing. Perchance it had only been a dream. Or maybe a stray dog outside or another drunkard staggering along the street.

A rattle and a slam of something sounded again, and she flinched. Whatever it was that startled her was still downstairs.

She cautiously tip-toed to the window. No one was on the boardwalk or in the street at this hour. The moon, shadowed partially by clouds, cast an eerie glow on the buildings across the street.

A pronounced thump reverberated below, and her shoulders tensed. What if whoever was downstairs attempted to break into her apartment? An intruder was not something McKenna thought she'd have to worry about in the small town of Hollow Creek. She worried regularly about Mother and Arrosa in Thorburn Flats, a dilapidated part of town in Missoula, but not here. Surely not.

She forced her feet to move. If whoever it was decided to bolt up the stairs, she would need to have something stronger than the door to protect her. With effort, she squatted and pushed the smaller trunk she used for her nightstand through the bedroom, bumbling along the uneven floor, and to the door. Out of breath, McKenna then searched for something to protect herself.

A cast iron skillet should do the trick.

Waiting in the dark shadows of the main room, she crouched low, the skillet at the ready. After several minutes, she darted to the front window and peered out once again. That's when she saw a man dashing across the street and into the night.

She returned to her place near the door. All was quiet now, except the pounding of her heart in her ears.

Light streamed through the windows the next morning. McKenna stretched from her cramped position and massaged the back of her neck. Why had she been sleeping on the floor? And why was there a skillet beside her?

She blinked and rubbed her eyes. After a few moments of foggy awareness, recollection took root. She'd heard a clamor downstairs and had positioned herself near the door in case whoever it was decided to visit the apartment next.

But had it only been a nightmare?

McKenna forced herself to her feet. The crick in her neck remained, and gooseflesh covered her arms. It wasn't a particularly crisp morning, but perhaps the nerves engulfing her caused the chill. She dressed, then prepared some coffee, taking a few minutes to inhale the delicious scent. If someone *was* in the boutique, were they still there? Ought she fetch Clayton before opening the shop? What if it was truly only a figment of her imagination? If so, she wouldn't want to pester Clayton. Oddly, his opinion mattered, and she didn't want him to think her a flibbertigibbet.

After breakfast, she rounded the edge of the building to the front. Passersby mingled on the boardwalk, enjoying the early summer day. She inhaled the crisp air and moseyed the few steps to the boutique when something caught her unaware.

The door was ajar, its lock apparently broken. Her heart thrummed in her chest, and she looked to the right, then the left. But no one paid her any mind as they bustled about their day. An automobile drove past and tooted his horn and a horse neighed.

McKenna slowly pushed open the door. Everything looked satisfactory from where she stood. She entered and took a gander about the room when she noticed something askew. Where was the necklace that was on the mannequin at the back near the additional room? Or the jewelry displayed in the far corner away from the view of passersby on the boardwalk? Or the bracelet behind the counter?

And with regards to the counter...what was that? She stepped closer. Inscribed in the wood were two chiseled scratches. Were they letters?

The weight of a stone settled in the pit of her stomach.

She'd been robbed.

"We'll keep searching for him. I sure wish I hadn't let him get away." Clayton kicked at a pebble with the toe of his boot.

"You had no way of knowing, son." Sheriff Volterman from Cullman County gripped his shoulder. "The main thing is we don't stop looking for Pietro Salazar until we find him."

The sheriff was right, and Clayton appreciated his support and encouragement. Once a month, they met to discuss the ongoings in their small adjoining counties.

Clayton rubbed his jaw. "I wonder why he supposedly stays in the area? With all the robberies, assaults, and murders he's committed, he should be halfway across the country by now to avoid being caught."

"Some criminals relish the thrill of staying one step ahead of the law. Could be the case for Salazar. He's an evil man, and there's no telling what goes on inside that thick skull of his."

"I'm just glad we haven't had to deal with him in Hollow Creek yet. The outskirts of town, yes, and then with me helping him three miles out, but so far the townsfolk haven't been at risk."

Volterman's forehead creased, adding to the map of wrinkles. "One thing that's telling and could potentially assist us in apprehending him is his telltale action with every crime."

"His telltale action?"

"You didn't know?"

Clayton shook his head. "Not sure I've heard of his telltale action. Was it on the wanted poster?"

"It's not. Figure they don't want common folk to know about what Salazar does each time. He inscribes his initials, *PS*, wherever he's been. When he robbed the train, we found his initials scratched on the safe. When he killed that man outside Missoula, he etched it in the front door of the man's house. And on and on. Not sure when he finds time to do that, but he does."

"He's a slick one."

"Indeed. We'll bring this fellow in and send him away for good if he's not hanged first. But best be careful. He's a dangerous man."

They bid each other goodbye, and Clayton started toward Hollow Creek. He'd visited Ma and spent the night before meeting Volterman early this morning five miles north of the border of Hollow Creek County. Pietro Salazar and his crimes weighed heavily on Clayton's mind. He'd arrested or assisted in arresting many criminals. Did his duty to keep the streets safe from the likes of Salazar. Determined to follow in Pa's footsteps and fight for justice. Lord willing, he'd do the same and stop Salazar's reign of terror on the towns and counties in Western Montana.

He cut across to a shortcut that saved him ample time. No sense in riding the prairie when he had a stack of new wanted posters, manure in the streets, and tax collection to be done. He rehashed first his meeting with Ma, then his visit with Volterman. The talk with Ma burdened him.

She was set on marrying Hal, and Hal was set on marrying her.

Prayer was in order for that situation as well as the one with Salazar. While Clayton liked Hal and knew he wouldn't do anything to hurt Ma, there was just something he couldn't accept about her replacing his father in her life.

Or *their* lives.

It took longer to reach Hollow Creek than usual. Perhaps maybe it just seemed that way given his lengthy list of matters to tend to. Clayton tethered his horse and entered the office. His lone occupant of the jail waved at him from behind bars.

"What is it?" he asked. He wasn't in the mood for the man's incessant questions.

"Some woman stopped by here earlier."

"A woman?"

"Yes. Pretty thang with blonde hair. Looked like she was half scared out of her wits. Said she needed to see you straightaway."

Bile slicked the back of his throat. What had frightened McKenna? Was she in danger?

"Did she say anything else?"

"Nope. Just wondered where you were. Looked like she mighta been cryin' or something."

"All right. Thanks." Without taking the time for the cup of coffee he so desperately thought he'd needed five minutes earlier, Clayton rushed out of the sheriff's office and to Miss Julia Mathilda's, all the while lifting a prayer to the Lord that something bad hadn't happened.

Three townsfolk attempted to stop him on his mission, and each time, he informed them he'd meet with them later today at the sheriff's office provided what they needed wasn't an emergency. His heart kicked up its heels the closer he got to the shop.

"McKenna?"

No one else was in the shop, and she rushed toward him. "Someone—" her chin trembled and her voice wavered.

And an alarm rang deep in his bones. "Did someone hurt you?" If someone hurt her, best they pray for the Good Lord's mercy.

"N—no."

Her shoulders shook, and he reached for her hand to steady her. Icy cold fingers met his grasp. "What happened?"

"Someone—someone last—last night robbed me."

"At your apartment?" His voice rose, and with effort, he tempered his fears.

"No. Here."

He exhaled a breath of relief. At least someone hadn't broken into her apartment and harmed her. A robbery, while bad, was something he could handle. "I'm so sorry, McKenna."

She leaned slightly into him. "All of the necklaces, bracelets, broaches, and some purses are gone. I—I've made a list." She gestured to the counter. "I was sleeping when I heard a noise last night. I was—I was hoping it was only my imagination."

He wanted to pull her to him and console her. To tell her he'd catch whoever did this. Instead, he reached up and gently swiped a tear that traveled down her cheek. "Do you remember anything else?" he asked.

"Just the loud noise, and that I was thankful whoever it was didn't come to the apartment next."

"Thank God it was only the shop he robbed."

Something he couldn't ascertain flashed across her face. She studied him for a moment, more tears streaking her cheeks before she added. "Do you think God stopped him from coming to the apartment?"

"Yes, I think the Lord was watching over you. The robber could have thought there was more jewelry upstairs, but for whatever reason didn't attempt to find out."

"What can be done?" Her voice rose an octave. "I can't pay for all that is missing, and I will lose my job over this."

He wasn't sure what exactly she meant by that statement other than she likely had to pay the vendor for the purchases—purchases she would not make an income for.

He would ask later. For now, Clayton needed to start gathering information and find whoever did this. Was it someone who worked alone? More than one person? Male or female? "I'd like to see the list. I'll also be looking around and seeing what other clues I can find. I saw Thad Evanson at the hardware store. Perhaps he'd be willing to fix the door for you."

"I would appreciate that."

"Do you remember or notice anything else that might be helpful?"

"Just that the person also scratched something into the counter."

Clayton's pulse ticked up a notch. "Scratched something?"

"Yes, like an inscription." She led him to the counter.

He angled himself from a few different directions, attempting to ascertain the hieroglyphics. It took him but a second. There was no doubt in his mind that Pietro Salazar had visited Miss Julia Mathilda's Fine Dresses last night.

CHAPTER FOURTEEN

SOME THINGS IN LIFE were completely unexpected. Take, for instance, Arrosa's illness, the mounting debt her family had accumulated, and Father's decision to embezzle. Or that McKenna would find herself in the uncivilized town of Hollow Creek.

But nothing was so unexpected as when Aunt Julia Mathilda strode through the doors of the boutique the following day without warning.

Was it wrong to keep what happened to herself until the items were recovered? If they ever were? To avoid sharing with her aunt that all of the jewelry and purses were gone? That while Clayton had a suspect, he had no idea where that suspect had gone or where the stolen items were?

Of course, if she kept such information to herself, Aunt Julia Mathilda would detect something was amiss and things would not bode well for McKenna. If such an event occurred last year, McKenna would have withdrawn money from her savings that Father added to each month. She'd repay Aunt Julia Mathilda and go about her days. But McKenna had no more savings account, and barring finding hidden treasure or discovering gold in the river, had no way of compensating her aunt for the goods that were filched.

A tightening sensation filled her chest as panic overcame her. Telling the truth was always the best course of action.

"Hello, McKenna." Aunt Julia Mathilda took her time wandering around the boutique before stopping directly in front of her.

"Hello, Aunt Julia Mathilda. What brings you to Hollow Creek?" She regretted her voice shook as she spoke.

"I can't very well send hundreds of dollars' worth of merchandise to another town and not inquire as to how it's selling, now can I?"

Her aunt had a valid point.

Aunt Julia Mathilda gestured about her. "While it's primitive and dismal, you have decorated it with some sense of taste."

"Thank you. I've enjoyed adorning what once was a dour and empty building."

"Hmm." Her aunt sashayed around the racks and settled near the mannequin in the window. "Whatever happened? I don't recall cracks in the mannequin's face before she was shipped here."

"Yes, I do apologize. She had an accident and crashed to the floor. The cracks have been glued, however, and unless one scrutinizes..."

Aunt Julia Mathilda held up a finger. "I didn't scrutinize, and I noticed. Now, do tell me, have you sold all of the jewelry? And the handbags? While I was just at the bank to check the deposit, it wasn't nearly substantial enough to have included the funds from selling the necklaces, bracelets, and brooches."

"I do need to discuss that with you."

Aunt Julia Mathilda pierced her with a hard stare, and McKenna grasped the edge of the counter to keep her weakening legs from toppling her over.

"What do you wish to discuss? And do make it efficient. I am to meet with Emilie Evanson for brunch."

McKenna peered outside the window. Townsfolk meandered along greeting each other and partaking in the warm day. Would someone walk in just as she conveyed to her aunt what happened?

"Do go ahead," prompted Aunt Julia Mathilda.

"Yes, well, the other night—in the middle of the night to be exact—someone robbed the store of its jewelry and purses." The temptation to squeeze her eyes tightly to avoid the glower she was likely to receive was great.

"Someone robbed the store?"

"Indeed. The sheriff is looking for the perpetrator, and Mr. Evanson arrived yesterday to fix the door."

"Wait. Do not speak another word." Aunt Julia Mathilda's chest rose and fell in rapid succession. "Do you mean to tell me that numerous dollars' worth of products are g—gone?"

"Yes. Unfortunately, but the sheriff..."

"I'll not hear another word. Either you replace the things stolen with money from your own wages, or find other employ."

"But, Aunt Julia Mathilda, you know I need those funds to send to Mother and Arrosa."

"It is not my fault your father accumulated a lot of debt and was unable to pay for it. It is not my fault Arrosa became ill. And it is certainly not my fault your father decided to *steal* to pay for his indiscretions of purchasing so many items he couldn't pay for. Those are his gaffes and his alone." She pursed her lips together and seethed a moment before continuing. "Moreover, it is not my fault my sister decided to marry your father. I always warned her *nothing* good would come of it."

Tears pooled in McKenna's eyes. "With all respect, Aunt Julia Mathilda, I will not allow you to speak of my mother and father in that manner. Father is a good man, he just made an error—one that he takes full responsibility for. Mother has good judgment, and marrying Father did produce something good. My sister." The sobs choked in her throat. Should she relieve herself of this job before being fired? Perhaps somewhere else in town would hire her. Maybe Mrs. Evanson would be willing to acquire another maid. Or better, yet, she could finally work with Mother in Missoula cleaning houses.

For a moment, she thought Aunt Julia Mathilda would soften as her voice lowered as she spoke. But it was not to be so. "Do you have any idea how hard I've worked to establish the boutique? It is not easy for a woman to succeed in business. As I mentioned previously, McKenna, either you pay for the items that were stolen from your own wages or I'll have no choice but to relieve you of your duties."

"Even if it wasn't my fault?" How could her aunt be so ungracious?

"Emilie Evanson's maid is arriving soon to retrieve me and deliver me to her home for brunch, so I best be on my way."

Without so much as another glance in McKenna's direction, her aunt left the shop, allowing the door to close loudly behind her.

Clayton was about to visit with McKenna about a slight, but hopeful, turn of events regarding the stolen items when he noticed a woman emerging from the shop looking none too happy.

"Ma'am, is everything all right?" he asked.

"Who are you and why is it your concern?"

He pointed to the badge pinned to his shirt. "My apologies. I'm Sheriff Clayton Beringer. I couldn't help but notice your irritation as you left Miss Julia Mathilda's Fine Dresses."

She narrowed her eyes at him and spoke through gritted teeth. "That is *my* business."

"What just happened is your business?" The woman did have a point. Perhaps he shouldn't have stuck his nose into her affairs.

"No, Sheriff. The shop is *my* business."

"The shop?"

"Yes. I am the proprietress of both it and the main boutique in Missoula. My niece, McKenna, manages the store here."

Clayton knew his jaw dropped near to his boots at the woman's words.

She continued. "And since you mentioned you were the sheriff, why have you not found the criminal who stole the jewelry and the handbags?"

"Ma'am, with all due respect, that happened just the other night. We are doing our best to locate the bandit and the goods he stole."

"See to it that you do."

"That is our aim. McKenna is beside herself with worry."

"As she should be."

Was the woman blaming the occurrence on her niece? "It wasn't her fault in any way. She locked the door, ensured that all expensive items were out of sight of those peering in the window, and took all necessary precautions. I'm grateful the outlaw didn't see fit to attempt to rob the apartment above the shop where she lives as well."

"I see." She swiveled her head back to the shop, then to Clayton. "Be that as it may, the stolen items are worth an exorbitant amount of money and *must* be found. I had no idea this was such a lawless place."

"Not that I'm in the habit of sharing information on a pending investigation, but our suspect has also committed crimes in

Missoula, including murder. Hollow Creek is considerably safer than the city."

"Hmm. Well, I best be on my way. Good day." She dismissed Clayton with a flick of her wrist and strolled toward Vera, who was driving Emilie Evanson's automobile.

Two customers entered the shop ahead of him, and Clayton loitered just inside the front door waiting to speak with McKenna. He didn't relish the thought of spending time in a woman's clothing store, and from the expressions on the two patrons' faces, they didn't believe he belonged there either.

But his mission for being there was twofold. To ensure McKenna was all right and to show her the wanted poster. For whatever reason, she wasn't as irritating as he'd once found her to be. While it was unlikely the women would notice something was amiss, Clayton could easily see from her slightly slouched shoulders and her reserved expression that something was wrong.

How could it not be? She'd lost an excessive amount of merchandise. Which brought him to another thought that clanged around his mind like a cowbell around the neck of a startled calf.

A haughty lady in her forties, whom Clayton did not recognize, narrowed her eyes at him as she brushed past. No man in their right mind would be in here, and yet he'd visited the shop numerous times.

Finally, both women left, and Clayton strode to the counter. The desperation in McKenna's blue eyes made him wish he had more substantial news than what he had to impart.

"Have you caught the bandit?"

"Not yet, but I do have some information."

"Oh?"

He positioned the wanted poster on the counter in front of her. "We believe this is the man who stole the items."

She gazed down at the paper, her brow crinkling. "I've never seen him before, but he sounds like an awful man."

"He is. He has a long list of crimes—theft is one of the more insignificant ones. Will you do me a favor?"

"Yes."

"If you see him anywhere or at any time, will you let me know immediately?"

She nodded, and he detected the sadness in her countenance. Had her aunt been as abrupt with her as she'd been with him? Should he ask? Did folks such as themselves discuss such things? He inwardly shrugged. Clayton supposed it could be part of the investigation—indirectly. He cleared his throat. "I met your aunt outside on the boardwalk. I had no idea she was here."

"Yes. I am managing it for her while she oversees the main boutique in Missoula."

"She said as much."

A few heartbeats ticked by while he waited for her to elaborate. When she didn't, he figured he might as well speak the thoughts on his mind. "She mentioned she's anxious for us to find the thief."

"She is." McKenna's shoulders slumped even more. "Unfortunately, I'm responsible for this shop and the items in it."

"But you're not responsible if someone steals those items. How could you be unless you were negligent in some way?"

Now he sounded like Pa. The thought made him square his own shoulders in pride. But as quickly as he did, he was reminded of McKenna's distress.

She opened her mouth to say something else, then abruptly closed it. Should he probe? He decided against it. "Try not to worry. It's our goal to find Salazar and recover everything he has stolen. Please remember that if you see him or if you have any other concerns, I'm just..." he gestured in the direction of the sheriff's office. "I'm just a few blocks away."

"I appreciate that. Thank you."

If only duty didn't call. If only he wasn't standing in a frou-frou shop with women's fancy shirts and dresses. If only he wasn't here on official sheriff business. He'd take more time to visit with her. To talk with her. To show her, as her new friend, that he cared.

McKenna appreciated Clayton's words of assurance. But such words wouldn't alleviate Aunt Julia Mathilda's demands that McKenna repay her for the stolen jewelry and purses. Why had she thought she could effectively manage the boutique? Why hadn't she instead gone to work cleaning houses with Mother?

The bell above the door jangled and Mrs. Arkley, the reverend's wife, and two other ladies from church entered. They oohed and aahed over several of the items just inside. "Hello, might I be of assistance?" Her voice sounded rote in her own ears.

But McKenna knew they could likely no more afford the finery in Miss Julia Mathilda's Fine Dresses than McKenna could apprehend the thief. A pang of guilt niggled through her. At one time not so long ago, she, Mother, and Arrosa perused the upper-class boutiques in Missoula—especially Aunt Julia Mathilda's—and purchased items to their hearts' content. At one time in the not-so-distant past, all three of them looked down their noses at women just like Mrs. Arkley and the other two women.

Bile pooled in the back of her throat. Had she really been so selfish?

"We have a favor to ask of you," said Mrs. Arkley, a broad smile lighting her face.

"Yes?"

"As you may be aware, the Hoekstra family lost their home recently to a fire."

"I was not aware. That's awful." McKenna searched her mind for any recognition of anyone in the Hoekstra family. But nothing registered familiarity.

"It is. We are praising God no one was injured or worse. Fortunately, they were not home at the time."

"Amen," chorused both of the other women.

"As such, we are seeking donations to assist them with rebuilding their home. We have already had some townsfolk donate the lumber, but we're in need of some other items. We'd also like to be able to purchase a few necessities since they lost everything. Would your business be able to help?"

McKenna's heart fell. She hadn't the funds to donate, but she knew what it was like to be homeless. She also knew that while it was likely Aunt Julia Mathilda had a benevolent fund, asking her after the robbery would be pointless and would only serve to remind her aunt of all that McKenna had lost for the business.

She was about to say that she regretted there was no way to help when she thought better of it. Coffee had been one of her few luxuries. If she did not purchase any coffee with her meager wages kept behind for herself, and forewent the new shoes she intended to purchase to replace her worn ones, then she could donate. Albeit not much as she couldn't take it from Mother and Arrosa, but it would be something.

McKenna opened her change purse and extracted all she had and handed it to Mrs. Arkley. "I regret it's not more, but I would be happy to donate my time in any way needed."

Mrs. Arkley squeezed McKenna's hand with both of hers. "Thank you so much. We would love to have you help us. By the way, if you'd ever like to join us for our Women's Bible and Missions Group, we'd love to have you. We meet on Wednesday mornings, mostly at the church, but other times at the homes of our members."

No one had ever invited McKenna to a women's Bible and missions group. Would they still want her in attendance if they knew how little she knew about God's Word? If they knew what Father had done? Before she could stop the flow of words, she answered, "That would be delightful. Thank you."

A thought struck her as she watched the women leave a few minutes later. While Arrosa was sick, Father was in jail, Mother's hands were chapped and peeled from overwork, and McKenna would be indebted to Aunt Julia Mathilda for the rest of her life for the stolen merchandise—provided she maintained her employment—the Hoekstra family had lost everything in the house fire and now had nowhere to live. For the first time that day, a joyful feeling flitted in her stomach.

She'd been able to bless someone else.

CHAPTER FIFTEEN

MCKENNA STOOD AT THE counter and wrote Mother a letter after she closed the boutique for the day.

Dearest Mother,
I hope you are doing well and that Arrosa continues to heal.

She tapped her pencil on the counter. Mother needn't know about the robbery because she'd only worry, but what if Aunt Julia Mathilda told her? It would be better for her to hear it from McKenna, and she *could* minimize it and still be truthful.

We've had such pleasant weather in Hollow Creek, but I hear we are in for a storm tonight. I still think of this town as primitive, but it's not as bad as I once thought. Are you still attending Pastor Shay's church? I attended one of the churches here last Sunday and have been endeavoring to read the Bible more.

It's been somewhat eventful at the boutique. Someone did steal some necklaces and purses, and the sheriff has been searching for the burglar. It sounds as though this person is one who steals quite often, so the sheriff is confident he will eventually be captured.

That sounded far better than how she could have described the crime. She wouldn't elaborate and mention that Clayton believed it to be a wanted criminal who had killed and assaulted others. McKenna shivered at the thought.

I miss you both dreadfully and hope to again visit at some juncture.

Unfortunately, the special discount for the new spur was no longer in effect. It would likely be some time before McKenna could again see her family. The thought discouraged her.

Aunt Julia Mathilda traveled here to see the shop.

She held the pencil in midair. Mother needn't know of her aunt's words about the stolen items. How Mother and Aunt Julia Mathilda were sisters remained a mystery since they were so very different.

Please say hello to Arrosa. I love you both so much and hope we will all be together as a family soon.
With love,
McKenna

She folded the letter, placed it in an envelope, and sealed it for tomorrow's trip to the post office. After closing the store, McKenna ascended up the stairs to the lonely and quiet apartment. Even in their mammoth mansion, she'd never felt so alone as she did in the paltry two-room rental.

That night, a fierce storm moved through the area, and McKenna huddled in her bed, blankets wrapped around her and pulled up tight to her chin. She'd never appreciated thunder, lightning, and hail. Even less so when she struggled with a myriad of emotions.

The first and foremost being how she would secure enough funds to both continue assisting Mother with supporting her and Arrosa *and* paying for Arrosa's doctor's visits, *and* paying for the missing merchandise.

The second on her mind was Father's upcoming trial. She'd heard stories about the prison in Deer Lodge. He would be sharing cell space with convicted murderers and others who had committed appalling crimes.

Much like this Pietro Salazar had committed according to the wanted poster Clayton showed her.

The man's image emerged again in her mind just as lightning flashed across the sky and lit up her small room. Hail started pinging against the window before it hit so hard McKenna feared the glass would break.

She shivered, pulled the blankets tighter around her shoulders and thought about what Mother had said about God's faithfulness. He had been faithful in protecting McKenna from this Salazar fellow. What if she had been downstairs at the time of the robbery? A man who murdered and assaulted would have no problem doing so again.

Father said God would take care of them that they needed only to trust.

One of the hymns they sang in church last Sunday talked of having a friend in Jesus.

Reverend Arkley said that God was their refuge. Psalm 46 confirmed it.

She attempted to reconcile all of these thoughts and reached for the Bible beside her bed. Perhaps reading more Psalms would help her understand. Once she read enough of them, she could pray and talk to God the way Pastor Shay and Reverend Arkley did. They spoke to Him as though He was Someone they could trust. Someone who was faithful. Someone who was a friend.

Tonight she would continue where she'd left off last night with Psalm 91. The second line reinforced what she'd read previously, "*I will say of the Lord, He is my refuge and my fortress: my God; in Him will I trust.*"

Had Father read this same verse and that's how he came to the conclusion about trust?

The wind howled, seeping through the cracks in the building and rattling the windows. She focused her attention on reading the remainder of the Psalm as more questions than answers formed in her mind.

Clayton rode to the Evanson Ranch the following day. One of Thad Evanson's hired hands, Jep, had fetched Clayton an hour prior.

And now, as he avoided mud puddles and remnants of hail that had not yet melted, he thought of how much he needed to accomplish today. He pondered whether what Thad had to say had any relation to another report he'd already heard and still needed to investigate.

When Wiley returned from the neighboring town, he'd solicit his aid. The first priority? Finding Salazar. If he was still in the area.

Likely the outlaw had already sold the jewelry and purses from McKenna's shop. The only good thing was that with the wanted poster disbursed to nearly every county in Montana and in counties in Idaho and Wyoming, there was a better chance of finding him. Clayton just hoped it was before the man committed further crimes.

Especially crimes against innocents.

Clayton met Thad and his foreman, Pete, by the barn. "Explain to me what happened. Jep didn't give many details."

"Our prize stallion was stolen last night during the storm."

"Are you certain he was stolen? Could he have run off?"

Thad shook his head. "He was secured and all of the rest of the horses are here."

"It's likely we didn't hear any commotion due to the storm," added Pete.

"The barn, unfortunately, is only 200 feet from the road, so it would be easy for someone to have taken him and left without anyone seeing anything. If the thief decided not to take the road, nothing would stop him from heading out in the opposite direction, cutting through the fields, and hiding in the mountains."

Thad's presumption was likely accurate. "But with the storm, I can't believe someone would get far. And wouldn't the stallion be skittish with the lightning and thunder?"

"Whoever it was had this planned," said Pete.

"I agree. Unfortunately, this is the second report I've received of a stolen horse. I was afraid that might be the case when Jep beckoned me."

Thad crossed his arms across his chest. "The problem is, this isn't just any stallion. It's worth a lot of money."

"I'm sorry, Thad. I promise we'll do whatever it takes to find it." Even as he said it, Clayton knew locating the horse would be a stretch. Someone could have ridden it to Missoula by now. "Were there any signs of someone entering the barn?"

"Not that I saw. You're welcome to look around," said Thad.

Clayton secured further information from Thad and Pete, then wandered around the barn where the stallion was formerly kept. He was about to leave when something caught his attention.

On the back of the barn door facing the interior, someone had carved something in the wood. He examined it more closely, then took a step back. He'd bet his own horse it was letters carved in the door, and not just any letters, but *PS*.

Next, he'd stop by the other ranch who'd reported a stolen horse.

Not only did he have a jewelry burglar on his hands, but also a horse thief. And he'd wager the culprit was one and the same.

And there was no doubt in his mind that culprit was none other than Pietro Salazar.

Pa always said solving two crimes in one made for a glorious day. Only this time, it would be three crimes, if only he could locate the outlaw.

Before he left, he stopped to speak with Thad again and tell him what he'd found.

"Before you go," said Thad, "I'm in need of another hired hand. Do you know of anyone who's looking for work?"

Clayton scratched his chin. He highly respected Thad and wanted only to suggest those he knew would do a capable job. Someone did come to mind. "Do you know Malachi Callahan?"

"Can't say as I've heard of him."

"He's about my age and new to Hollow Creek."

"Upstanding citizen?"

"I believe he's doing his best and that everyone deserves a second chance. He recently had a skirmish with the law—the only one I know of due to a fight he was in because someone attempted to steal his pocket watch."

Thad arched an eyebrow. "But you would vouch for him?"

"I would."

"Thank you, Sheriff." Thad extended a hand, and Clayton shook it. "And thank you for coming out here today. I appreciate all you're doing for the town and the county."

McKenna finished redressing one of the mannequins when Emilie Evanson entered the boutique. "My, you have it looking so nice in here."

"Thank you." Those words would have meant the world to her if Aunt Julia Mathilda had said them.

"I am so grateful Julia Mathilda opened a boutique here. Not that I mind traveling to Missoula—but this is far more convenient."

McKenna smiled. "I'm thankful my aunt decided to open a shop here as well." And she was, with the exception of having to fret about the stolen items.

"So how are things going? Are you adjusting to Hollow Creek?"

"I am. At first, I thought it to be backwards and uncivilized, but I'm now of the mind to favor it over Missoula." That and no one here knew of Father's crime.

"Oh, yes, I understand completely. I was much the same. But now there's no place I'd rather live."

Mrs. Evanson could live anywhere with her wealth, and she chose to live here?

"Mrs. Arkley told me she invited you to come to one of our Women's Bible and Missions Group meetings. We'd love to have you."

McKenna picked a thread from her shirtwaist. "I appreciated her invitation."

"No obligation to do so, but I think you'd be an excellent fit for our group. The ladies are delightful and so welcoming. For the longest time, I was quite lonely here and yearned for fellowship. Most of my dear friends live in other towns in Montana.

When Mrs. Arkley invited me to join, I was hesitant, but now I'm so glad I did."

"Thank you, Mrs. Evanson, but I'm not well-versed in the Bible." The words slipped out before she could stop them, and she put a hand to her lips. What would the woman think?

"Nor was I. There is much to learn in God's Word, and I'm confident Reverend Arkley would tell you he still hasn't learned all there is to learn."

"But he's a pastor."

"Indeed. Pastor Shay in Missoula, whose church we frequent when visiting the city, would say it takes more than a lifetime to learn all of the gems hidden within the Good Book's pages."

Pastor Shay? "I've met him. He was so kind in assisting..." Mrs. Evanson needn't know McKenna's family was destitute and the reason for it.

"He is kind. And do call me Emilie. Now, I have two reasons for frequenting the boutique today. First, I must find a new dress for a trip to Missoula Thad and I are taking this weekend."

"We have many new lovely ones." Grateful for the change in topic, McKenna led Emilie to a rack with elegant garments from the most recent trunks.

"Oh, yes, these are elegant." Emilie chose a silk evening dress and an afternoon gown in white with blue ribbons accenting the waist and neck and carried them to the counter. "Now for the other reason for my visit. Your aunt discussed with me the other day while dining at my house for the noonday meal that you had been robbed."

"Yes."

"I'm so sorry to hear that. One of our most valuable stallions was stolen during the storm. It's an unsettling feeling to be the victim of a robbery."

"Yes, it is."

Compassion shone in Emilie's amber eyes. "I mean no disrespect when I say this, but Julia Mathilda's decision to hold you responsible for the theft is not a position I agree with. I did mention such to her, graciously, of course." Emilie reached across the counter and patted McKenna's arm. "Whatever jewelry and handbags Sheriff Beringer is unable to locate, I will personally pay for."

McKenna's mouth fell open. Had she heard correctly? She inhaled a deep breath. "While I am ever so grateful, I cannot allow you to pay for the stolen items."

"Well, if they are not recovered, I insist." Emilie offered a smile that matched the kindness in her voice.

Emotion filled McKenna's chest. "Thank you so much."

"You're more than welcome."

"God provides." She voiced Pastor Shay's words even as Mother's words about God being faithful echoed through her mind.

"Yes, He does."

McKenna worried her lip. "Might I confide in you?"

"Certainly."

She peered about the boutique, empty except for her and Emilie. Dare she express the nagging questions in her heart? "I—well—I don't know much about the Lord. You see, my family only attended church on Christmas and Easter, and I am embarrassed to say I didn't listen much to what Reverend Metzger said, even though I recall it sounding rote."

"Interesting you mention that. My family was much the same. I didn't surrender my life to Christ until just last year."

"Last year?"

A slow smile alighted on her face. "Yes. I do believe you and I are what could be referred to as kindred spirits in many ways.

It sounds as though we grew up in similar fashion and that we both experienced a hunger for the Lord just recently."

McKenna had no idea what Emilie meant when she said she'd surrendered her life to Christ. "I have been attempting to read the Bible every night. Do you think if I do it with dedication and full commitment without fail and if I learn how to pray as Reverend Arkley does, that the Lord will be faithful to me? That He will take care of my family and provide what we need?"

"You can't earn the Lord's love, faithfulness, and provision." There was no judgment in Emilie's words, only compassion in her eyes.

"But if I can't earn it, then how will I ever experience it? I want so badly for my sister to be healed from her illness and for Mother to..." she stopped short. She didn't know Emilie well enough to share all that burdened her.

"Do you remember when I offered to pay for the stolen merchandise?"

"Yes." Was Emilie having second thoughts?

"Did you do anything to earn my favor in doing so?"

"N—no."

"Exactly. My decision to reimburse your aunt for the jewelry and handbags stolen by an outlaw is a gift. You couldn't earn it. I just gave it."

McKenna was more confused than ever. The thoughts emerging in her mind couldn't be spoken quickly enough. "But I want so badly to believe God is faithful as my mother says; that He will provide as Pastor Shay mentioned; that He will take care of us if we trust, according to my father; that He is our refuge as Reverend Arkley preached; and that Jesus is our friend and anything can be taken to Him in prayer as we sang in the hymn." She took a deep breath.

"He does and is all those things. And yes, He wants you to spend time in His Word learning more about Him and joining in fellowship at church and worshipping Him. But doing all those things will not earn His love, for that is a gift just like the gift I'm giving you should the merchandise not be recovered."

They spoke at length for the next hour, Emilie patiently answering McKenna's questions and suggesting she speak with Reverend Arkley about the many inquiries McKenna expressed that Emilie did not know the answer to.

McKenna promised to do so and was grateful for Emilie imparting so much wisdom. But the thing she was grateful for the most? That Emilie patiently taught her that day what it meant to surrender her life to Christ.

After Emilie left, she locked the door and hurried to the apartment to retrieve a piece of stationery. Once again in the boutique, she started a letter to Mother and Arrosa in between customers and store duties. For how could she keep the excitement about all that Emilie had shared to herself?

Chapter Sixteen

McKenna peeked out the boutique window Saturday morning just as Tippi and Ophie parked the red automobile near the boardwalk.

Oh, how she'd anticipated a break from the mundane! Temporary relief from thoughts of the burglary, worries about her family, and the dismal solitude the apartment offered. To spend time with friends as she so often had in Missoula.

Before friends could no longer be found and had determined the Chapman family below their station.

As a matter of fact, she'd barely been able to sleep last night just thinking about going for a ride in Tippi and Ophie's parents' Buick. To travel by motorcar once again. To go for a drive in the open air as she once did when Father would take the family for Sunday drives.

The weather was perfect for it, too.

She dashed from the shop, being mindful to lock the door behind her, and nearly flew into the backseat.

"I thought you'd never get here," she said, her words breathless through all of the excitement.

Tippi pulled the motorcar from its parking spot and started down the street. "Father was slightly hesitant."

"Slightly?" asked Ophie. "More like significantly. Utterly. Extremely."

McKenna leaned forward. "Why the hesitation?"

"He doesn't think Tippi is a good driver."

Tippi removed a hand from the steering wheel and jabbed her sister. "He's the one who taught me. He knows I'm a cautious driver and far better than you."

"Humph. Well, he only allowed you to drive because you're older. Always the older one who gets the privileges around here." Ophie folded her hands across her chest, and from her profile, McKenna could see she was pouting.

"Oh, look!" Tippi swerved to the right and waved with one hand.

McKenna focused her attention on Clayton and Deputy Toolin walking along the boardwalk. They both waved, and her gaze caught Clayton's.

Or at least she thought he was looking her way. Her heart stuttered. My, but he was a handsome man with his tan shirt, jeans, and cowboy hat.

"Isn't he just dapper?" Tippi gushed.

"Yes, he is," McKenna agreed, then immediately thought better of sharing her thoughts about Clayton with Tippi and Ophie. She liked them, but some things were private.

Tippi put on the brakes and stopped in the middle of the road. She whipped her head around so fast that McKenna thought she might have given herself a headache.

"You think Wiley is dapper too?" Her tone spoke of panic, her eyes widened, and she clutched the steering wheel.

"Wiley?"

"Yes. Deputy Toolin."

"Oh, Wiley. No. I don't."

"Are you sure?" Tippi's voice rose an octave.

Ophie giggled. "This could end your friendship. Tippi has been fond of Wiley for at least a year."

"Oh, I'm not fond of Wiley. Nor do I think he's dapper." While it was the truth, the way the words flew from her mouth could cause the sisters some suspicion as to the accuracy of her statement.

"You don't think he's dapper?" This time, Tippi's eyes not only widened, but bulged. "Why, he's the most handsome man in all of Montana. Or most likely the United States."

A plume of dust filled the air as a wagon passed them. "Best you keep driving rather than stopping in the street," suggested Ophie. "Someone is liable to tell Father you are an incompetent driver."

McKenna rested a hand on her new friend's shoulder. "Don't worry, Tippi. I do not find Wiley dapper the way you do. But he's a handsome gent for you."

Relief flooded Tippi's countenance, and her tense shoulders relaxed. "That's fantastic to know. Thank you. I really appreciate our friendship, and for a moment, I feared we were both fond of the same man." She again faced forward and drove the car down the street.

Ophie slouched in her seat. "Shall we commence going on our drive now that we have that matter settled?"

"Yes, oh, bossy one. But first..." She put on the brakes again and whipped around once again. "If you don't think Wiley is handsome, who then?"

"Your brain is so muddled with thoughts of Wiley that you're a birdbrained flibbertigibbet." Ophie shook her head. "Of course, she's talking about the sheriff."

"The sheriff?" Tippi's jaw went slack.

McKenna felt the heat rush up her face. "I—well—"

"He's so tall and large-shouldered." Tippi scrunched her nose. "I much prefer..."

"Narrow sloping shoulders and a man of shorter stature? Yes, Tippi, we know." Ophie waved at a passerby. "Now can we continue on our drive? I'd like to see more than just the first two blocks of Hollow Creek."

"You're just jealous, Ophie, because there's no one for you to fancy in this backwards town."

"Au contraire. I'm not jealous at all." Ophie swiveled and faced McKenna. "Tippi much prefers men who could blow away with a slight sneeze."

"Such audacity! That is not true. Wiley is a brawny man with formidable strength. Why do you think he's so effective at capturing outlaws?"

"Brawny and with formidable strength? I guess I just don't see it. What about you, McKenna? Do you think Wiley fits that description?"

"Well..." she leaned back and lounged in the comfortable seat.

"Choose your words carefully, my friend," teased Tippi. "It's a long way back to town."

Ophie rested her arm on the black leather armrest. "Yes, three blocks, but who's taking note?"

McKenna didn't wish to upset her friend, but in her opinion, Wiley was not brawny. She recalled the time he'd assisted Clayton with the trunks. Formidable strength? No. She gazed behind them and noticed that both men had stopped on the boardwalk and were talking with another gentleman. Tippi might much prefer Wiley's appearance, but McKenna found Clayton to be quite dapper.

And when exactly had that happened?

Oh, she'd noticed him from the first time she'd met him. Noticed him when he'd lugged the trunks up the stairs. When he'd trapped a criminal in the boutique. When he'd assisted her after the robbery. At church. And all the other times before, after, and in between.

"Don't you think, McKenna?" Tippi was asking.

"Begging your pardon?"

"I was just asking your thoughts on the beautiful wildflowers. It's such a lovely time of year."

"Indeed." The blue vervain, violets, periwinkle, fireweed, yellow coneflower, and Indian paintbrush all lined the sides of the road as they left town. While she'd been all over the world, there wasn't a place she'd rather live than in Montana.

Listening to Tippi and Ophie prattle on in the front seat caused an ache to lurk in her ribs. An ache for Arrosa and the close relationship they shared. She missed her sister and their abundant conversations and, at times, arguments. Would Arrosa ever feel well enough again to partake in some of the activities they once enjoyed?

Even now, McKenna was grateful for the time away from the loneliness of the apartment. Having lived a life of constantly attending societal events, balls, plays at the theater, charity fundraisers, and the like, days with only work to occupy her time were foreign. Thankfully, she'd become immediate friends with Tippi and Ophie, and they never questioned her station in life, although they were of high-class with their father being a prominent rancher in the area and their mother consistently arranging charities.

A thought entered her mind, and she again inclined forward and edged her shoulders between the sisters. "Do your parents find it acceptable that you fancy Wiley given he is below your station?"

Ophie snorted an unladylike snort. "When they first found out, Father nearly had a conniption and Mother suffered from a moment of hysteria."

"That was because they didn't know."

"Know what?" asked McKenna.

"You know how it is, McKenna. We are expected to find someone who can keep us in our extravagant lifestyle. Someone who won't squander away our family fortune but rather add to it."

McKenna recalled that from years past. Now, however, there was no extravagant lifestyle and no family fortune to squander. If she'd cottoned to someone like Clayton before her family had lost everything, would her father have had a conniption and her mother lapse into hysteria? Quite possibly so. "Yes," she answered, knowing the sisters expected a reply. They assumed her to be of considerable wealth, and she'd not express to them otherwise for fear they may not maintain their friendship with her.

Just like Kathy, Ellen, and Priscilla hadn't. The hurt wedged itself in her heart so deeply that she pressed a hand to her chest, the pain still fresh. McKenna had cried a fair amount about their disloyalty.

"So, thankfully, Wiley's parents are of wealth. He's just one of those independent sorts who has always wanted to be a lawman." Tippi shrugged, causing the automobile to swerve to the left. "I think they, as well as our parents, believe Wiley will someday be finished saving the world and seeking justice. He'll then be able to settle down and be a suitable husband."

"When you're both in your fifties," sputtered Ophie.

"No commentary necessary, Ophelia Harkins. You'd do well to find yourself such a fine fellow as Wiley is. What about you, McKenna? Is there a man who has captured your fancy in Hollow Creek? Besides the sheriff, of course, since he's far below your station, and to our knowledge does not have wealthy parents."

Clayton *had* captured her fancy, but that was all the further it would go. She'd keep her fondness for him to herself as such a pairing would never succeed, wealth notwithstanding since she had none herself.

"No, no one here."

"How about in Missoula? I bet there are so many handsome men there." Ophie swooned, and McKenna watched as she swayed in the seat from side to side.

She pendulated in such an exaggerated motion with her hand to her bosom that she collided with Tippi's arm. The Buick zigzagged from one side of the road to the other while Tippi attempted to maintain control.

The deer standing in the middle of the road didn't help.

Tippi swerved and the motorcar left the road and bumbled along in the field, jostling its passengers about. "Hold on!" shouted Ophie.

McKenna clutched the armrest and willed her backside to stay put in the seat.

"Oh, dear!" Tippi's discombobulated cries sounded above the hum of the automobile's engine.

"Father's going to kill you." Ophie's voice reverberated in a shrill response.

And McKenna now gripped the armrests on both sides as hard as she could. The basket of food beside her for their picnic bounced out and landed on the uneven ground.

"You need to stop this thing!"

"Thank you, oh, bossy one. I'm trying!"

Finally, the automobile came to a stop and lurched them forward.

They sat in silence for several seconds. The vehicle's back end slid backward, and the front end tilted upward in the ravine.

"Father is really going to kill you," Ophie muttered again.

Tippi elbowed her. "No sense in making me feel worse."

"Can I have all of your dresses, books, and jewelry?"

"I'm bequeathing nothing to you." Tippi shot her sister a narrowed gaze. "Oh, dear. What do we do now?"

"We should probably get help," suggested McKenna. Her heart wouldn't stop racing in her chest. They could have been killed, although she'd not mention that to Tippi, who was sobbing and leaning her head against the steering wheel.

"It's been a good life," she sputtered. "I'm only twenty-four, but it's been a full and good life."

McKenna released her right hand from the white-knuckled grip on the armrest and set it on Tippi's shoulder, hoping to provide some sense of comfort. "Perhaps we can seek assistance."

Tippi shook her head in a rather dramatic motion. "There is no help out here. None at all. We're miles from town."

"I wouldn't say miles. Maybe *a* mile," countered Ophie. "But there is an awful lot of mud everywhere. Before we return the automobile, we best wipe it off."

Ophie was correct. Flecks of mud dotted the once-shiny black leather seats, and the hood boasted mud freckles. Not to mention McKenna's own pale blue shirtwaist was no longer just pale blue.

"I'm not even worried about the mud caked on it. I'm only worried about liberating it from the ravine."

Birds chirped and the scent of wildflowers lingered in the air. McKenna cast a glance behind her, in front of her, and to both sides. They weren't far from the road. "Perhaps we could walk to town and garner some help."

"From whom?" Tippi wailed.

"You mentioned earlier that Wiley had insurmountable strength. Perhaps he and Cla—Sheriff Beringer might be able to free us from our predicament."

"I can't bear the thought of seeing Father's face. Mother will insist I never drive again. She was already against the whole idea until I reminded her that Emilie Evanson and her hired help, Vera, drive all the time." Tippi wailed. "Whatever will we do?"

Little had she known her friend's flair for the dramatic. "At least we weren't injured. It could have been worse."

The Lord is faithful.

The words pressed on her mind unannounced. They could have been badly injured. They could have hit one of the trees. They could have overturned the horseless carriage.

"I'll walk to town and fetch help," she offered.

"All right," squeaked Tippi. "Take Ophie with you for protection."

The wanted poster Clayton had shown her flashed in her mind. While they were likely only a mile from Hollow Creek and most passersby—if any were on the deserted road—would be kindly folks from town, one could never be too cautious. Even if petite Ophie would offer minimal security. "Will you be fine here?"

"Yes. I'll be considering my demise."

Ophie rolled her eyes. "You never know. Just because it's his favorite possession, Father may forgive you. You might be disowned, but he'll probably forgive you."

"I daresay you're not helping, Ophie Harkins."

McKenna braced a foot on the running board and a hand on the flared red fender as she guided herself from the vehicle. Unfortunately, her foot slipped and she landed face down in the damp weeds.

CHAPTER SEVENTEEN

BEING A SHERIFF WAS not for the faint of heart. You just never knew what you might see or what might be asked of you.

He'd just finished locking the cell behind the drunk and disorderly man and had attempted to return to his cup of cold coffee when he saw a sight out the window he'd not soon forget.

McKenna, mud splattered on her clothes and face and accompanied by Ophie Harkins, staggered down the boardwalk. He sprang from his seat and hurried toward them. "Is everything all right?"

He had the urge to reach up and gently brush aside some of that caked mud on her lovely face, but he restrained himself. Initial order of business was to determine if she or anyone else was injured or in danger.

"We need your help."

"Is anyone injured or in danger?" The first two questions every lawman should ask, according to Pa.

"No, nothing except perhaps McKenna's pride." Ophie covered her mouth with her hand and sniggered.

In response, McKenna brushed the skirt with her hands. He noticed a red blush covering her face—well, the parts of it not covered in dried mud, anyhow. She dipped her head.

It crossed his mind that he might be a besotted fool. When had he initially taken notice of McKenna? Well, truth be told, he'd *noticed* her the day he'd first laid eyes on her. And then while carrying up the trunks, and the first time she'd laughed. And the time she'd cried after the burglary and when she sat beside him in church, and how pretty she always looked with her blonde hair, blue eyes, and slender form...

"Sheriff?"

Ophie's words interrupted his thoughts. "I, uh, sorry. What is the matter, ladies?" He straightened his shoulders and puffed out his chest. No matter what might be of concern to them or what predicament they'd found themselves in, he was here to offer his assistance.

"Might you help us pull the automobile from the ravine?"

"Pardon?"

Ophie, always the obliging sort, offered to translate. "You see, the automobile somehow found itself in the ravine about a mile from here. Perhaps Wiley could aid us in retrieving it. Is he somewhere in the vicinity?"

"The automobile is in the ravine?" Clayton reluctantly tore his gaze from McKenna and stroked his cleanshaven chin. "It just happened to find itself there?"

"Exactly."

"You could fetch your father, or I could. He'd know best what to do. After all, this is his prized motorcar."

"Don't we know it? Tippi is planning her funeral as we speak since she was the one driving."

"But she's not injured?"

"No, sir."

"And you, McKenna, are you injured?"

She lifted her eyes to his and his breathing briefly stalled. "No. I'm fine and appreciate your concern. Tippi is worried about her father finding out so we were hoping you could help us retrieve it, Tippi and Ophie could drive it home, and all would be well. Perhaps her father wouldn't be the wiser."

"We would need Wiley's help as well. Tippi insisted." Ophie spun her head in all directions as if Wiley was hiding in some nook or cranny in the cramped sheriff's office. She waved a hand over her face. "Pee-yoo! What is that smell?"

"Likely one or both of the prisoners. As for Wiley, he's at the hardware store, and we'll fetch him on the way."

Wiley was more than happy to assist. That didn't surprise Clayton. He knew the man fancied Tippi Harkins. Good thing his family had affluence. While he liked Mr. and Mrs. Harkins and they did much for the community and pledged their allegiance in voting for him, they would not condone Tippi marrying a destitute lawman.

And that is exactly what Wiley would be if he didn't have the family fortune, because spending money, especially on books, was a favorite pastime.

After securing two more horses from the livery, the four of them prepared to ride to the location where the motorcar had "found itself in the ravine."

"Just please don't tell Father, whatever you do," insisted Ophie.

"Don't worry. We'd never do such a thing. No sense in getting Tippi into trouble." Wiley nodded at Clayton. "Do you think we will need to fetch more men for this rescue plan?"

Clayton hadn't really considered all of the ramifications of the matter. It wasn't like he rescued an automobile out from a ravine everyday.

His thoughts turned to McKenna, who rode beside him. Her hair tousled in the breeze, and his gaze remained fixed on her. That was until a near-miss with an oncoming wagon reminded him that if he didn't want his horse to have the same future as the Buick, he best pay attention.

Wiley was prattling on about something or other, and Ophie was pointing at scenery along the way as if she were a tourist guide.

They passed one other automobile and two men on horseback before they approached a sight that would embed itself in Clayton's mind for the foreseeable future. The 1910 red Buick Surrey—Mr. Harkins's pride and joy delivered all the way from Flint, Michigan—was lodged in the ravine, front end up. He heard Tippi's sobs before he saw her bent over the steering wheel, head in her arms.

He ventured to say that even if he and Wiley were successful in getting them out of this predicament, Tippi wouldn't be driving the Buick again anytime soon.

"Not sure how we're going to remedy this situation," said Wiley. "Any suggestions, boss?"

Wiley only called him "boss" when they were about to encounter danger or he was clueless about a solution. Clayton surmised today it was the latter.

He dismounted then assisted McKenna from her horse and gently righted her on the ground. Her hair tickled his nose, and he inhaled the scent that reminded him of flowers on a summer day. Everything about this woman, from the time he'd met her, had been unexpected. Especially his growing feelings for her.

For a moment their gazes connected, and he couldn't tear his eyes from her lovely face.

"Clayton?"

Wiley's voice interrupted the pleasant moment, and Clayton reluctantly tore his eyes from McKenna. "Might be that we need more help than just us."

"No, please," begged Tippi. "We can't allow anyone to know. Can you imagine if word got back to Father?"

Clayton didn't want to state the obvious—that Mr. Harkins would likely realize his prized motorcar was not in the same condition now as it was when it left his sizable ranch earlier today. He pondered their options. "Well, we could tie the horses to the front, one of you ladies..." he looked from McKenna, to Ophie, to the inconsolable Tippi. "McKenna and Ophie could lead the horses, and Wiley and I could assist with pushing the Buick."

At that, Tippi's distraught mood lifted. "Ooh, that's a fantastic idea. And Wiley would be remarkable at liberating the automobile from its location."

One would have to be blind not to see the swooning Tippi was doing over Wiley. Swooning he returned. Those two. If they weren't married within a year, Clayton wasn't the sheriff of Hollow Creek County, Montana.

"Thankfully the tall weeds should help us gain some traction. We need all the help we can get."

His idea to bring along two shovels was a good one. While the thick weeds precluded too much digging, any way they could obtain some leverage was deemed beneficial. Wiley headed to the left side. Problem with his deputy was that with his skinny stature and lack of muscle, it was akin to one and a half men rescuing the Buick instead of two.

After digging, they tossed the shovels aside. Clayton attached the rope to the suspension and prompted McKenna and Ophie to lead the horses at the count of three, and at the same time, he and Wiley would push the car, one of them on each side.

Tippi stood a few feet away wringing her hands.

"All right, here we go—one, two, three!" The simultaneous pushing and pulling nudged the automobile forward in the knee-high weeds, but not enough to heave it out of the ravine. Whether Tippi liked it or not, there was a strong possibility he'd have to head to town and get more help.

His boots slipped and slid on the wet vegetation, and mud flung up from the motorcar's tires.

"Man down!"

"Wiley? You all right?"

Clayton told the women to stop, and he waded through the weeds to the other side where Wiley struggled to pull himself up off the ground by clutching to the running board of the Buick.

"Oh, Wiley, how dreadful. You could have been killed or worse." Tippi plodded through the field to stand beside the man who'd obviously won her affection.

Wiley stood, attempting to brush off his jeans to no avail. "I was nearly dragged when the automobile began to move," he said, as if telling a story to an audience.

"It's fortunate you are such a capable fellow and so strong to be able to hold on tightly to the car. I hazard to think of you being swept beneath the tires."

Wiley offered a brusque nod. "It's never a safe day for a lawman."

Clayton chuckled. Wiley and Tippi were perfect for each other. And perfect for the Hollow Creek Theater —if there was one.

After a brief interlude, they attempted again. This time, the Buick rolled farther and almost up the ravine.

"You got it, you got it!" Ophie shouted from her place at the front of the motorcar. "Oops, but goodness. Guess you don't got

167

it," she said with a mock accent as the automobile rolled back down the ravine.

Clayton figured he'd found new muscles in his shoulders, arms, and legs—ones he'd never before used. "Let's take a break for a minute," he said. McKenna was comforting Tippi, who was beside herself with worry. He hated to have to, as they say, be the bearer of bad news. "Tippi?"

She looked up at him with red-rimmed eyes. Perhaps Wiley would be better suited to deliver their bleak options.

"Please don't tell me we must find more people to help us." She sniffled, and Clayton again wondered if she'd ever considered a career in the theater.

"There may be no other way."

Ophie slung an arm around her. "Don't worry, Tippi. If Father disowns you, we have relatives in Topeka you could stay with."

That obviously did not waylay Tippi's fears.

"Clayton, could we talk in private for a moment?" Wiley asked, and Clayton followed him away from the women.

"What is it?"

"I can't stand the thought of Tippi being upset. Can we try one more time?"

"We can, but I'm not sure it will do any good."

Wiley nudged him. "We have to at least attempt it. For Tippi."

They walked back to the Buick. "We can try again. Tippi, this time you sit in the automobile, crank the engine, and slowly drive it as we're pulling."

"I can do that," she squeaked and crawled into the right-hand side of the horseless carriage.

Clayton rolled his shoulders and Wiley cracked his knuckles. This time the Buick budged. Once at the top of the shallow ravine, Tippi shut off the engine, climbed out, and rushed to

Wiley and gushed, "Thank you so much, Wiley. I knew you were remarkably strong."

CHAPTER EIGHTEEN

FORTUNATELY FOR TIPPI AND Ophie, the automobile wasn't broken, or at least from what Clayton and Deputy Toolin could tell. After the debacle, Tippi drove McKenna and Ophie back to town, their picnic lunch long forgotten. They parked in front of the mercantile, and the deputy purchased several cloths to clean the muddied exterior.

Passersby stopped and stared. Would one of them share with Mr. Harkins about the condition of the horseless carriage? For Tippi's sake, McKenna hoped not. As she assisted with the cleaning duties, she thought of how, while the day had taken a vastly different turn than she'd expected, McKenna enjoyed her time with the sisters. While they filled a temporary void of friendship, she missed Arrosa all the more. Perhaps someday when her sister healed, Arrosa could visit Hollow Creek. Oh, what a joy that would be!

Sometime later, she bid Tippi and Ophie goodbye, and Deputy Toolin mentioned he had some patrolling to do.

Clayton turned to her. "It's been a long day. Would you care to meet at the restaurant for supper?"

But what of her dirt-smudged dress and face? "That sounds like a grand idea. Might I stop by the apartment first?"

"I'll retrieve you in a half hour."

McKenna rushed up the stairs to the apartment. In her former life in Missoula, she would draw four or five afternoon dresses from her wardrobe and spend an hour trying each on just to find the right dress for the occasion. Such was not the case now, as she owned only her faded clothes, one Sunday best, and the four Aunt Julia Mathilda purchased for her to wear at the boutique. She chose her favorite—a white shirtwaist with eyelet lace and a cornflower blue skirt. After cleaning the mud from her face and arms, McKenna pulled on the skirt and buttoned the shirtwaist before fixing her hair.

Why she wanted to look her best for Clayton was beyond her.

Well, maybe not *so* beyond her. Yes, she was growing fond of him.

Exactly a half hour later, he offered his elbow, and she accepted as they walked to the lone restaurant in Hollow Creek, a delightful establishment known as Olga's Café. McKenna had only passed by and peered in the window and had yet to partake in a meal there.

Until today.

The aroma alone when they entered caused her stomach to rumble, and she placed a hand on it, willing it to quiet. Oh, how long it had been since she dined in a restaurant! The waitress led them to a table in the corner, and Clayton pulled out her chair before sitting in his own across from her. The waitress brought them each a glass of lemon soda, and McKenna perused the menu while doing her best not to appear overeager. Fare that didn't consist of bread, oatmeal, or eggs sounded delightful. Not that she'd ever complain since she knew firsthand any sustenance was something to be grateful for.

"Never thought I'd be called to remove a motorcar from a ravine," said Clayton, interrupting her thoughts about food and the excitement that trilled within her at seeing peach pie on the menu.

"Nor had I imagined riding in a motorcar that found its way into the ravine."

He chuckled and their eyes met, causing her heart to pitter-patter against her ribcage. "I honestly don't think it will be long before Wiley and Tippi announce their courtship. He's been fond of her for a while yet."

"And Tippi certainly fancies Wiley."

Was it proper etiquette to discuss such matters? When she courted Leonard, their conversations centered mostly on the weather, Leonard's university days and subsequent employment, and newsworthy events found in the local paper. How very different the two men were. She felt much more at ease visiting with Clayton even though she'd known him for far less time.

The waitress returned to take their orders. "I would like the roast turkey with cranberry sauce, boiled potatoes, and peach pie, please."

"And for you?"

Clayton tapped his chin. "I'll take the usual."

"Roast spring lamb, cucumbers, and sponge cake." The waitress verified his choices and wrote them on the paper with McKenna's order. "That will be served momentarily."

"Have you any news on the theft?"

Clayton shook his head. "No one has seen Salazar, but we do suspect him in another crime, so it's believed he's still in the vicinity."

"Another crime?"

"Yes, the Evansons and the Strothmans each had a horse stolen during the storm the other night."

"Oh, yes. Emilie mentioned such when she visited the boutique." Thoughts of the discussion McKenna shared with Emilie and the subsequent excitement of now being part of God's family thrummed through her. She hoped to muster the courage to attend the Women's Bible and Mission Group at some juncture.

They discussed the shop, Clayton's job, and the fact that Hollow Creek was growing in comfortable camaraderie before the waitress returned with their meals. The roast turkey smelled heavenly, and McKenna leaned forward and inhaled the steam rising from the potatoes.

Clayton folded his hands to say grace, and McKenna mirrored him. His prayer was much as Reverend Arkley's and Pastor Shay's. Sincere, grateful, humble, and worshipful. The types of prayers she'd like to someday pray. "How did you learn how to pray?"

He shrugged. "Faith has always been important to my parents, and I guess I never really thought about it. From the time I was a young'un, my parents and I prayed for our meals, as well as at night before bed and other times during the day. He's my Heavenly Father, and I reckon having a pa I loved and respected made it easy and comfortable for me to talk to God." He regarded her for a moment. Did he realize she was new in her faith? That she'd stumbled and bumbled along when talking to the Lord? "Are you close with your pa?"

"I am. Are you?"

"I was. I lost him when I was twelve. He died while working as a sheriff in Cullman County."

"I'm so sorry."

Clayton placed his napkin in his lap. "Thank you. I miss him everyday. Is your pa in Missoula?"

"Yes—no." She couldn't tell a lawman Father was in jail awaiting a sentence that could land him in prison due to a foolish decision.

"He once lived in Missoula?" His smirk told her he was joshing her.

Thankfully, the waitress returned to refill their glasses with lemon soda. They discussed other topics, including extended family, of which Clayton mentioned he only had one uncle—his mother's brother—a lawyer in Missoula.

That news pricked her ears. While there were plentiful attorneys in Missoula, there were none Father could afford, so one did donate his time. However, he had a substantial amount of cases, so the attorney's efforts were lackluster to say the least. Dare she ask what type of law Clayton's relative practiced? She set her fork on the table and dabbed at the corners of her mouth. "What type of law is your uncle's specialty? Does he assist those who are incarcerated?"

Clayton listed several areas of law his uncle practiced, none of which included her father's dilemma. "Why do you ask?"

"I just know someone who is too poor to retain a lawyer but is in jail awaiting sentencing. He's sorry for his mistakes and hopes to stay out of Deer Lodge."

"What kind of crime did he commit?"

"Embezzlement."

"I see."

Did Clayton believe one deserved a second chance? That perhaps one could remain in a county jail rather than be sent to Deer Lodge to serve his time? "He believes fully in paying his debt to society and paying back all he owes to the business he stole from. However, he has a family and would prefer to remain in the Bleakney jail." Memories of Father in the dreary cell flashed through her mind, and a wave of emotion engulfed her. She dipped her chin and focused on the last few bites of her peach pie. "He has fully admitted his guilt and knows he broke the trust of the company from whom he stole, as well as his family. He's not asking to be released, as he knows he must serve his time, he's only asking not to be sent to Deer Lodge." Her voice shook, and she realized the peach pie no longer held the appeal it once had.

"Do you know this man well?"

How could she answer that? Father was one of the people she loved most in this world. "Yes, I do."

The scent of baked bread lingered on the air as the waitress delivered biscuits and gravy to a patron nearby. Utensils clanked, folks carried on conversations, and the waitress cleared their plates.

"I can certainly ask him if he'd help your friend."

"Thank you."

Clayton's brow furrowed. "I will see him when he visits Ma next week. He travels from Missoula from time to time, and with the spur recently completed, that will become more frequent. Do you have a name that I could give him so he could look into the matter? My Uncle Art is a charitable fellow, and I know he'll ask."

She moistened her lips and blinked through the moisture in her eyes before lifting her gaze to his. "It's my father."

Of all the people she could have mentioned, Clayton hadn't been expecting that answer. His first thought was perhaps a beau, maybe a brother, or even a cousin. But her pa? He was the one in jail in Bleakney for embezzlement?

From her distraught expression, he should have known it was someone close to her. What were the details? When had it happened? Why had her father chosen to steal?

For the next several minutes, he asked all of the questions that lingered in his mind, and as they prepared to leave, one thing stuck in his mind.

He would do what it took to convince his uncle to assist Mr. Chapman.

CHAPTER NINETEEN

SHE HADN'T SLEPT WELL the past few nights after telling Clayton about Father. While he reassured her he'd speak with his uncle, who sounded like a benevolent sort, McKenna wasn't sure she should have mentioned it at all.

Spending time with Clayton had caused her to appreciate the friendship that had unexpectedly bloomed between them. Would her revelation change things? She'd stared up at the ceiling last night, awkwardly asking the Lord for two things. First, that if there was some way Clayton would not think less of her for being the daughter of a criminal, could that be so? And secondly and more importantly, that his uncle would consider representing Father. She'd stumbled along with her words, whispering them aloud in the darkness of the night. Everyone's prayers that she'd heard in recent days included giving thanks to God. So, she'd done that as well. Thanking Him for Arrosa's slow improvement, Mother's good health so she could work, McKenna's employment at the boutique, and for her new life in Jesus. As she floundered along with her words, the praying became somewhat easier.

The following day, McKenna bid her most recent customer goodbye when a familiar face caught her attention. Aunt Julia Mathilda, followed by four men carrying two trunks, entered the boutique.

Her heart stalled for a moment. Would her aunt chastise her because the thief had not yet been found? Because the jewelry and purses had not yet been recovered?

"Just set those..." her aunt scanned the small shop. "I suppose, just set those right there." She pointed the only available spot to place anything, a narrow aisle-way between two clothing racks.

Four men, two of them McKenna recognized as ones she'd seen before in town, one she'd never seen, and the last who looked vaguely familiar—although McKenna couldn't place from where—did as Aunt Julia Mathilda requested. She handed them some money. "Return in an hour, haul the trunks back to the train station, and I'll pay you the rest." She waved them away, and they scuttled out of the store.

McKenna held her breath and mentally evaluated whether or not she ought to be forthright and tell her aunt about the lack of news regarding the missing items. She gripped the counter and braced herself for what was to come. If more goods were being delivered, perhaps that was a good indication she would maintain her employ. However, it could also mean...

Her aunt marched toward her. Weariness tugged at the corners of her eyes, and for the first time, McKenna noticed the exhaustion in her countenance. "How are you, McKenna?"

"I'm well. And you?"

"The past few days have been nothing short of arduous, but other than that, I'm well." Aunt Julia Mathilda regarded her. "As you can see, I've brought two more trunks brimming with wares. There are mostly dresses to replace the ones you've been selling but also a few necklaces and handbags."

"Are you sure..." McKenna swallowed the knot in her throat. "Are you sure you want to leave any jewelry here, what with..."

"Have you had requests for jewelry?"

"Yes, but—"

"Indeed. A clerk cannot run a successful boutique if she does not keep her shelves stocked." She swiveled her head from left to right. Would she notice the thin layer of dust on the far shelf that McKenna hadn't yet found time to clean?

"It's apparent the shelves and racks are becoming bare."

McKenna had been grateful for the influx of customers in the past two weeks. Much of it had to do with Emilie bringing her out-of-town friends into town for an outing three days ago. They'd stopped at Olga's Café for the noonday meal, then partook in an afternoon of shopping with cost being no barrier to what they wanted.

Just as cost had been no barrier once upon a time for McKenna's family. She unconsciously peered down at her scuffed shoes and swished her skirt over the boots as best as she could.

"McKenna..."

Aunt Julia Mathilda took another step toward her and grasped McKenna's cold hands in her own. "I have much to say today, but first I must apologize for my untoward behavior last time I visited this primitive town."

It was with great effort that McKenna not allow her jaw to drop at her aunt's statement.

"I was reminded twice of the unfavorable way I dealt with you regarding the robbery. First while I dined with Emilie Evanson. She reminded me the theft was not your fault. Secondly, when I was at a customer's home in Missoula this past week, your mother was there cleaning." Aunt Julia Mathilda dropped McKenna's hands and diverted her eyes to the floor. "I daresay I've never seen my sister in that capacity." Her voice hitched.

McKenna's eyes burned with tears as she thought of Mother working so hard for so little so she and Arrosa could survive. The walking to and from the homes of affluent customers, sometimes in hot weather as she returned home to their dreary apartment in Thorburn Flats. Her chapped knuckles, tired face, and slumped shoulders.

Oh, Mother. If only I could do more.

Aunt Julia Mathilda cleared her throat. "Be that as it may, we all have our lot in life. After I left and your mother finished, we met in the nearby park to chat briefly before my next appointment."

As on so many occasions, McKenna struggled with reconciling the fact that her mother and aunt were sisters. They were so opposite, even when McKenna's family was affluent. Of course, she and Arrosa contrasted each other in appearance. McKenna was blonde and blue-eyed like Mother, and Arrosa, auburn-haired and hazel-eyed like Father. But their personalities were far more similar than Mother's and Aunt Julia Mathilda's.

"Your mother didn't know much about the robbery. I surmised you didn't wish to worry her, so I minimized the seriousness of it. After I reassured her you were fine, she repeated what Emilie had said—that you were not to blame. Needless to say, a sizable conviction rose in my chest. And here I was, blaming you and demanding you repay the funds lost." Her aunt rolled a bony shoulder and pressed the wrinkles from her expensive dress. "Has your mother ever spoken about our childhood?"

It took McKenna a moment to recover from her aunt's words. Never had she seen this much humility. "I—no, not much. Other than you were from a wealthy family in Missoula."

"Indeed. When our parents passed, I took my portion of the inheritance and opened the shop. It wasn't easy, even with the generous funds I was allotted. I've worked hard for every dime I've made, and even harder for respect amongst the business community." Aunt Julia Mathilda sighed. "Having the boutique was one way I could perhaps measure up to your mother."

"Measure up to Mother?" While prior to Father's embezzlement, one might consider both women successful, Aunt Julia Mathilda was far more prosperous now. In the eyes of the world, anyhow. From what McKenna was learning about the Lord, His ways and His measure of success and prosperity were vastly opposite from that of the world. While she couldn't grasp it all yet, she did know that in His eyes, because she was His, she was wealthier than even the richest person. In His eyes, because she had her loving family, she was more prosperous than one with affluence but no family, or a family who shared no love and loyalty.

"Your mother and I are close in age just as you and Arrosa are, and she the eldest by a mere margin. When we were young, she was the beautiful one. The popular one. The one whose dance card was always filled. She had the better figure and the prettier hair while I was tall, gangly, awkward, and homely. I wasn't surprised when she married first, although your father was not the first to propose. Your mother had a substantial list of potential suitors who would do just about anything to win her hand. Meanwhile, there was no one seeking courtship—and definitely not marriage—with a plain, boring, and dull woman such as myself. It was no surprise, then, that I would become a spinster while your mother would go on to marry, have two children, and live in one of the most prestigious neighborhoods in Missoula."

For perhaps the first time, McKenna felt compassion for her aunt. She placed a hand on her arm. "I'm so sorry."

"Yes, well, at the time, despondency filled me to the utmost, but as time went on and I developed a mind for business, I realized we all have different courses our lives take, whether we prefer those courses or not. As such, I fear losing the business because it is all I have."

"But that's not true, Aunt Julia Mathilda. You have us—Mother, Father, Arrosa, and me. We love and care about you."

Tears glistened in her aunt's eyes. "Well, thank you. I do need to seek your forgiveness for my harsh and brash manner when I saw you last."

"I forgive you." What was that sermon Reverend Arkley preached about last Sunday? Something about forgiving people seventy times seven times? She'd have to research it in her Bible this evening.

"Thank you." Aunt Julia Mathilda lifted her shoulders. "Now, there is work to be done, and no sense in dwelling on gloomy thoughts. Let's unload the trunks. I believe we might find something in there for you."

"For me?"

"Indeed. But we'll not discover what that is if we stand here dawdling. I'll assist you with the trunks, as after they are emptied, they will be loaded onto the train headed for Missoula tonight. I'll also be catching today's last train, but I trust you'll do just fine arranging all of the new merchandise."

Suddenly, McKenna's heart felt lighter. While Emilie Evanson had offered to pay for the jewelry and purses, McKenna still held hope that the items would be found. And if they weren't? At least she would no longer have to repay Aunt Julia Mathilda for them.

"God is faithful."

"God will take care of us. We need only to trust."

Her parents' words again entered her mind, along with the words of her now-favorite Psalm. *"God is our refuge and strength, a very present help in trouble."*

Indeed, He had been her strength, and this occurrence with Aunt Julia Mathilda could be considered nothing short of a miracle.

It was halfway through unloading the second trunk when her aunt clasped her hands together. "And there they are," she proclaimed.

McKenna tilted her head in the direction her aunt indicated just as Aunt Julia Mathilda removed a pair of the most gorgeous, patent leather lace-up Ackhurst Lady's Boots with a bow on the front. "These are for you. Do try them on posthaste."

She did not need any further convincing. McKenna slipped off her raggedy boots and donned the new ones. "These are marvelous and just what I hoped they would be!" She stood, twirled, and walked on high heels to the edge of the boutique and back, thankful no customers were about.

"And you look elegant and well-attired," declared Aunt Julia Mathilda.

"Thank you so much." She enveloped her aunt in a hug, and only after a few seconds of the embrace did she notice Aunt Julia Mathilda had stiffened.

"Do forgive me, dear. I'm not accustomed to such a display of affection."

McKenna released her and sashayed around the crowded boutique one more time. "Thank you for the boots and thank you for the dresses." She thought of the dresses her aunt had previously graciously given her on the pretense that a woman should only look her finest when managing Miss Julia Mathilda's Fine Dresses.

Dresses she would not have had were it not for her aunt's generosity, for McKenna owned only a few garments since all else had been purloined when her family lost everything to pay back the bank.

Sometime later, the men returned to transport the trunks back to the train station, but McKenna scarcely noticed as she was spending the last remaining minutes with her aunt before she bid her farewell.

CHAPTER TWENTY

MISSOULA BOASTED A PERMANENT telephone exchange in 1891, and someday Rocky Mountain Bell would install a telephone in Hollow Creek. According to an article in the last week's newspaper, that "someday" for Hollow Creek would be within the next year.

Thinking about how much easier it would be to conduct business with a telephone exchange, Clayton read the letter from his uncle.

Clayton,

I would be happy to assist Mr. Chapman with his legal case at no cost. Thank you for bringing him to my attention as I attempt to aid someone each year. I will visit him in the Bleakney Jail and see what can be done for him. Hope all is going well for you and your ma. For what it's worth, I liked Hal when I met him recently. I think he'll do right by your mother.

Uncle Art

Clayton folded the letter and tucked it into his shirt pocket. Likely his uncle had already visited Mr. Chapman. Clayton would remember to pray for his uncle for guidance. While he didn't know the entire story behind McKenna's pa's incarceration, he did wager that it had taken a tremendous toll on her family. And as fond of her as he was growing, he didn't want her to face undue hardship.

He stopped into Olga's Café for the noonday meal and ordered his usual. He'd spoken to several ranchers in the area and showed them Salazar's photo on the wanted poster. Then he visited with folks in town. Only one person recognized Salazar so far, and that was because he'd seen him in passing last month.

An hour later, Clayton and Sheriff Volterman from Cullman County sat in his office planning their strategy for finding Pietro Salazar. Clayton's deputies, including Wiley and Ivinson, were patrolling towns in the county and would be apprised at a meeting later today.

"It's obvious it's Salazar," said Volterman. "He's a sly one. Thieving right under our noses. Yesterday he assaulted an innocent man who just happened upon him. The man will recover, but it'll take time what with broken ribs and a stab wound."

That could very well have been the situation for Clayton that day he stopped to unknowingly assist the outlaw. The Good Lord was certainly watching over him. "He needs to be stopped. Let's hope we can recover all he's stolen—or what we suspect he's stolen so far."

Volterman stroked his graying beard. "I spoke to the sheriff in Missoula a few days ago, and they've seen no sign of him. I'm surprised the man isn't halfway to Mexico by now, but I'm confident he's in one of our counties."

"It's just a matter of time before we haul him in."

"I like your way of thinking, son. Your pa would have been proud."

Clayton hoped so. "Thank you, sir. It means a lot to hear that coming from you." He'd always admired and respected Volterman, the man who'd once upon a time been one of Pa's four deputies before running for sheriff and being elected and re-elected several times over.

They were continuing their conversation when Malachi Callahan entered the building. "Sheriff, can I speak with you for a minute?"

"Hello, Callahan, come on in."

Volterman stood and gestured to his formerly occupied chair.

"If it's all the same to you, I'd rather stand." He paced a moment, then settled in front of Clayton. Tightness bordered his eyes, and he rubbed the back of his neck.

"Is there something we can assist you with?"

Callahan picked at a nail. "Yes, there is." His gaze darted between Clayton and Volterman before finally settling on Clayton. "I've been doing some random ranch work until I find a steady job. I was riding the area past Perritt's place yesterday when I stumbled on something I think you ought to know."

Clayton leaned forward and steepled his fingers. "Go on."

"There's an old neglected barn thereabouts that hasn't been used recently, as far as I can tell. Anyhow, I thought I heard something, so I went to investigate. Out there in the middle of nowhere in that barn with no one around were two horses. I'd bet this month's wages they are the stolen ones that disappeared from those two ranches here. There was a stallion and the other a blue roan Percheron mare. Both are quality horseflesh."

Volterman met Clayton's eye, and Clayton knew they were thinking the same thing. "Thank you for this information, Callahan. We think you may have just helped us solve a crime." He nodded to Volterman, and they both grabbed their hats before bidding Callahan goodbye.

"Do you think he's part of the thefts?" Volterman asked when they left the sheriff's office. "He sure was nervous."

"I don't think he is. Callahan is a good man. He's struggling a bit, I reckon, but he's trying to do his best. And yes, a nervous sort, but that was likely due to stumbling upon the horses like he did."

Volterman agreed, and they rode to Perritt's place. Clayton prayed they'd find the horses in good health and that if they were, in fact, the ones that were stolen, that they'd soon be returned to their rightful owners.

Several days passed since Aunt Julia Mathilda delivered the latest trunks and her aunt made amends. With business increasing as of late, McKenna still needed to properly organize the store including the additions of the newest merchandise.

She draped a stylish peach-colored dress over the counter and pressed any wrinkles out from its time in the trunk. All of the gorgeous items held her spellbound. She had taken so much for granted.

McKenna displayed the three necklaces, one of them pearl, on the back shelf away from prying eyes looking through the window. One of them, a locket, drew her attention. She ran a finger over the oval-shaped cameo necklace. It reminded her of the one she once owned with a photograph of Mother and Father on one side and one of Arrosa on the other. Her parents presented it to her as a gift for her eleventh birthday.

That too had been confiscated to reimburse the bank for the thousands of dollars Father had embezzled. Funds that went to pay for the extravagant lifestyle her parents could not afford, even with Father's lucrative position at the bank and the immense wealth her parents inherited.

Emilie mentioned that nothing happened beyond the Lord's knowledge. This presented numerous questions in McKenna's mind, questions she would be asking likely into old age. For instance, if He knew something was going to happen, why didn't He stop it? Arrosa might then never have fallen ill. She shoved aside the thoughts for now. There would be ample time to inquire as to the answers to the numerous plaguing questions.

One thing she did know was that since surrendering her life to Christ, she yearned to know more and more about Him.

So involved in decorating the boutique with the latest items, McKenna failed to realize the hour. She again pondered her aunt's declaration. Never before had she seen Aunt Julia Mathilda express such humility. Her own heart felt lighter than it had in months.

While McKenna had become accustomed to the apartment, she wished there was direct access to it from the shop, rather than her having to walk clear around to the back of the building and up the rickety steps. Summertime didn't present a problem, but she cringed at the thought of plodding through the snow and ice and gripping the handrail so as not to fall. Or the cold winter evenings when darkness came early. She'd not delight in traipsing through the murkiness into the isolated alleyway to the back door.

She locked the store and meandered down the deserted boardwalk. Most folks were eating supper at this hour or preparing to retire for the evening. All of the businesses—save the two saloons—were closed, and the sun slipped lower in the sky as it approached sunset in a couple of hours.

As McKenna rounded the corner and slipped into the alleyway, a hand, seemingly from nowhere, clutched her arm and jerked her nearly plumb off her feet. She teetered to one side before haphazardly righting herself, but the tight grasp on her arm remained.

A hand clamped over her mouth before she could give voice to her befuddled thoughts. Her heart stalled. What had just happened?

She angled her neck to the right. A man whose features were vaguely familiar glared at her.

A shriek rose in her throat, muffled by the hand, and she winced at the pain extending from her upper arm down to her hand.

"Don't scream. Don't say a word or you'll find a bullet in your back."

His hand disappeared from her mouth before the shiny metal of a revolver glinted in the lingering shadows and pressed against her side.

"Why are you doing this?"

"Shut up," he growled.

She may not have recognized him initially, but now his features were clear.

Pietro Salazar's dark eyes bored into her.

Her trembling legs made it difficult to stay upright as he dragged her toward a horse tethered in the alley.

McKenna whispered a prayer and peered about her. Surely someone would be about. The barrel of the gun dug deeper into her side. "Get on the horse."

"You won't get away with this."

He cocked the hammer of the gun. "Don't speak. Get on the horse."

The foul odor of laundry long unlaundered stung her nostrils. With difficulty, she did as she was told, her legs threatening to collapse as she mounted the horse. He climbed on behind her, this time shoving the barrel into her back.

"Where are we going?" Her shaky voice sounded in her ears, and her heartbeat pounded so forcefully, her chest ached.

"We're going to Missoula where you will take me to the place that keeps bringing you all the jewelry."

To Missoula? "N—no."

Mr. Salazar clutched a wad of her hair and yanked back her neck. She heard a pop, and the pain radiated down into her shoulders. "You won't tell me what we will and won't do," he snarled. "Now, if we should see someone, you say nothing unless you want to die."

But if he killed her, how would he steal from Aunt Julia Mathilda's Fine Dresses in Missoula? She might prevent a crime, but in exchange, she'd give her life.

Dizziness swirled around her, and she trembled, the quivering becoming more pronounced as they rode through the alleyway and cut across the far end of the town. She was new—so new at praying—but during a recent sermon, Reverend Arkley reinforced what Clayton insinuated when he said one could talk to her Heavenly Father just as she did her earthly father. *"He longs for you to come to Him with any concern in your heart."*

She recalled her favorite verse that she'd now memorized: *"God is our refuge and strength, a very present help in trouble. Therefore will not we fear, though the earth be removed, and though the mountains be carried into the midst of the sea; Though the waters thereof roar and be troubled, though the mountains shake with the swelling thereof."* The reminder that the Lord was her refuge and there for her in trouble calmed her somewhat.

Lord, I don't know what to do. Please help me.

Pietro Salazar nudged the horse to the outskirts of town. The farther they rode, the more remote the chances of someone rescuing her.

"You are a pretty woman," he hissed in her ear.

An involuntary shudder rippled through her and bile rose in her throat. There was no telling what horrible things Mr. Salazar might do to her if she did not flee from her abductor.

Quick, McKenna, think!

But her mind clouded with images of Mother, Father, and Arrosa. The pain this would cause them.

No. She would escape. She *must* escape.

Against her natural inclination, she squared her shoulders and did her best to scan her surroundings for someone—anyone—who might help.

Then she saw him.

Her answer to prayer.

Clayton was patrolling the area just ahead. Pietro Salazar veered the horse in the opposite direction, but not before McKenna yelled as loudly as she could, "Missoula!"

He thumped her hard on the side of the head. "I told you to shut up!"

Tears brimmed in her eyes. She didn't want to die. Didn't want to leave her family behind. Didn't want to miss a possible chance of finding her one true love with the man she'd grown fond of in recent days.

Had Clayton even heard her? Would he understand what she'd said? Would Pietro Salazar harm him if he came to her rescue?

Lord, please. I don't know how to pray. But please, please help me. Please let Clayton have seen and heard me, and please keep him safe.

Mr. Salazar prompted the horse faster. If Clayton had not heard her and was not in pursuit, she must think of an alternative plan. But what? Escape when Pietro Salazar fell asleep? Somehow render her assailant unconscious? But how? She had no weapon. Unless...

Suddenly, Mr. Salazar turned and shot at something behind them. *No!* The voice in her head sounded alarm bells. Was Clayton behind them? Had he been hit?

They rode much too fast through forested trails with tree branches occasionally slapping at them as Mr. Salazar paid no heed to safety. Finally, after climbing for several minutes, he abruptly stopped the horse.

"Get off!"

He didn't wait for her to respond, but instead jerked her from the saddle. She fell hard on the pine-needle-covered ground, her knee jarring as she did so. He yanked her by the arm until she stood. Her right leg quivered and nearly gave out due to the fall, and her heartbeat pounded in her ears as Mr. Salazar dragged her through the dirt. Why had they stopped?

McKenna's question was answered seconds later when she saw Clayton inching his way through the trees. She gasped a prayer of thanks that he had not been injured by Mr. Salazar's previous shot.

Her captor took aim, and Clayton ducked behind the trunk of a thick cottonwood. "Let her go, Salazar!"

The man shot at the tree trunk, the loud roar of the gunshot sounding in her ears. She caught a distinct whiff of the scent of gunpowder. The shot ricocheted off the trunk, and Mr. Salazar fired again.

"Let her go and we'll do this just between the two of us." Clayton's voice echoed through the trees, and she exhaled a breath of relief. Until the man fired several more rounds in the same direction. If she were free to run, would she even be able to with her legs frozen to the spot where she stood? Beads of sweat dampened her forehead. Never had she felt so helpless.

Hello again, Lord. Can you please keep Clayton safe, and can you please help me to know what to do?

When Mr. Salazar paused to reload his revolver, she took the opportunity.

Stomping as hard as she could with her pointed-heeled boots, she aimed for Mr. Salazar's instep. He winced, grabbed a handful of her hair, and again yanked her head viciously to the side. Pain shot through her neck and down her shoulders.

Seemingly from out of nowhere, Clayton appeared and shoved her captor to the ground. McKenna tottered to the side before tripping over an exposed tree root. Clayton and Mr. Salazar sparred, their wrestling causing one, then the other to gain the upper hand. Fists pounded. Her heart constricted. Where was Mr. Salazar's gun?

The answer came soon enough when she noticed he still held it in his hand. Clayton pounded on the man's wrist, forcing him to release it.

"Run, McKenna!"

But she couldn't. Not when Clayton was in danger and not when her legs refused to move.

She must do something. Anything.

Without the wherewithal to stop herself, she stumbled forward as the ache in her knee and neck reminded her of her injuries. When Mr. Salazar had again gained the upper hand, she lifted her left leg and kicked him as hard as he could in the side. She heard him gasp. Without wasting a second, she then brought her heel down on the back of his knee.

The distraction gave Clayton just enough time to regain his strength and point his gun directly at Mr. Salazar. The outlaw reached up and attempted to remove the revolver from Clayton's hand. Clayton's arm shook as the much larger Pietro Salazar attempted to wrest it from him.

A gunshot sounded through the forest, and McKenna's breath caught.

CHAPTER TWENTY-ONE

PIETRO SALAZAR WASN'T LONG for this world, whether because he didn't survive the gunshot wound or due to the punishment likely meted out by the judge. After the outlaw was transported to the infirmary and Clayton wrote his report of all that had occurred, he again lifted his eyes heavenward and thanked the Lord.

Things could have gone so badly. Had he not been delayed by the arrest of a rowdy drunkard, he might have finished his duties early, moved on to another chore, and missed Salazar kidnapping McKenna altogether.

The Lord was truly watching out for the woman who'd claimed his heart. He rested his pencil on the desk, checked on his lone prisoner who was mumbling something incoherent under his breath, and struggled to his feet. Doc said his injuries—mainly bruising—would heal in time, but for now, Clayton compared himself to a ninety-six-year-old man with his painful and lethargic movements.

More importantly, McKenna's physical injuries were minor as well. Doc told her to stay off her feet for a few days to allow her knee to heal, and he dispensed McBride's Nerve and Bone Liniment for both her knee and neck injury and laudanum for the pain.

McKenna. She invaded his thoughts on a constant basis now, and he shuddered to think he could have lost her. If he hadn't been patrolling, if he hadn't seen her and heard her scream "Missoula", likely indicating that was where Salazar intended to take her if God hadn't given Clayton the upper hand in the skirmish and the ability to be a sure-shot when he fired the pistol.

After the gunshot that incapacitated Salazar, she ran to his arms and he'd held her close. Her hair, much of it having fallen from its bun, hung to her shoulders. Clayton gently patted the back of her head and pulled her even closer, hoping to envelop her in the safety of his arms.

He hadn't wanted to release her—she felt perfect in his arms as though she belonged there. When she took a step back and peered up at him, relief in her gaze, an odd feeling struck him in the center of his chest.

He was in love with McKenna Chapman.

Lest he consider himself a besotted dolt like Wiley, Clayton shook off the smitten thoughts and, with a struggle, returned his contemplations to the outlaw who had wreaked havoc on three counties.

Once Salazar regained consciousness, Clayton had some questions for him. Namely, about the missing stallions and the jewelry. His was more than a hunch that the man was involved in all three thefts. Wiley would return Monday, and Sheriff Volterman from Cullman County and the sheriff from Missoula County would be joining him for a joint investigation and to hopefully locate the stolen goods.

If those goods could be located.

Tomorrow after church, he and McKenna would go for a drive. Their social stations were far different, so he had deliberated about even allowing himself to fall in love with her.

Too late, Beringer.

The door opened and Rantz stomped through, allowing it to slam behind him.

Clayton rubbed his bruised temples. Rantz had the worst timing, although no timing would be agreeable when it came to this particular adversary.

Rantz lifted the chair, turned it around backward, and dropped into the chair with a huff.

"What do you want, Rantz?"

"I'll tell you what I want." He pointed a finger at Clayton. "You ought to be removed from office immediately what with how you handled apprehending Salazar."

Most would tell Clayton he did a remarkable job, which of course was the Lord's doing. "Let's have this conversation later."

Rantz pounded the desk with a closed fist, causing Clayton's report to jump. "I will not have this conversation later. Resign immediately."

"What? So you can take my place? Isn't that what you want? Besides, I followed proper protocol."

"If proper protocol is putting a civilian in harm's way."

"I rescued her."

"This ain't the Wild West anymore."

Clayton could beg to differ since they lived in rural Montana, but he held his tongue. Meanwhile, Rantz narrowed his eyes, a pulse twitched in his jaw, and he inclined his head as if daring Clayton to argue.

Clayton's head throbbed, his ribs ached, and he was concerned about McKenna's neck and knee. He didn't need Rantz's nonsense, and he was about to tell him as much when the door opened and Hal walked in. The older man looked from Clayton to Rantz, then back to Clayton again. "Rantz, are you here harrassing Clayton?"

"Not your business," Rantz sneered.

"It is my business. Now why don't you mosey along and find something else to do with your time instead of causing trouble at every turn?"

Rantz stomped toward Hal and stood face-to-face with him, sizing him up. Rantz fisted his palms at his sides. "Ain't no one asked you to intervene."

Hal didn't flinch. "What seems to be the problem?"

"This so-called sheriff here didn't handle a case properly."

Clayton was about to interject when Hal voiced his thoughts. "You look here, Rantz. You won't find a better sheriff than Clayton, unless, of course, you consider his pa. He cares about the townsfolk and cares about justice. If you don't like the job he's doing, run for sheriff yourself."

Rantz's shoulders shook. "I have."

"And you lost. Twice. That should tell you something. Go spend your time doing something productive and leave Clayton alone unless you want to be thrown in a cell for disorderly conduct." Hal nodded toward the door.

Rantz turned to Clayton, opened his mouth, then quickly shut it before tromping out of the building.

"Thank you, Hal."

Hal gripped his shoulder. "You're welcome, son. Doubtful your pa would allow someone to talk to you that way and nor will I."

Clayton appreciated Hal's loyalty. The concern and serious-ness in his kind eyes told of his sincerity, and Clayton's chest tightened. He'd been unfair to the man who cared not only about his ma but also cared about him.

"Thank you."

A grin twitched on Hal's face, causing his mustache to lift and the deep wrinkles in his face to become more prominent. "I would defend you anytime, Clayton. I think you're a dedicated sheriff and are doing an outstanding job protecting the county."

"I appreciate that." He wanted to say more, but the words stuck in his throat.

"Well, I best get to my appointment with a cattle buyer, one of my reasons for traveling to Hollow Creek today besides stopping in to say hello. You have a good day." Hal nodded and left the sheriff's office. As Clayton watched him go, something inside him stirred.

Maybe he ought to give Hal a chance.

Clayton accompanied McKenna to the Evanson Ranch the following Saturday for a welcome home party for the newest addition to the Evanson family.

Numerous wagons, automobiles, and horses filled the driveway. The plush green grounds surrounded by trees, black-eyed Susans and numerous other varieties of flowers, and abundant ranchland dotted with cattle greeted them. The Bitterroot Mountains rose in the background, providing a breathtaking scene.

With the exception of the cattle and mountains, this might have been her family's home. Homesickness stirred McKenna's heart. With effort, she reminded herself that it wasn't the house that made a family, but a family that made the house, no matter what that house looked like, even if it was an apartment in Thorburn Flats.

Clayton offered his elbow, which she accepted. Such was becoming natural these days. If only things were different. Perhaps another time and place, they might have courtship in their future. But she doubted a man of the law would date a woman whose father was on the opposite side of it. At least they were at the same station in society.

She peered up at his profile—a profile she'd grown fond of in the short time of knowing him. Clayton Beringer was a handsome man, kind, and gracious too. And he loved the Lord. That had never mattered to McKenna before. Not when she'd courted Leonard and not when she'd entertained the thought of marriage with one of the numerous suitors seeking her hand before Father's downfall.

Vera greeted them when they entered, and McKenna concluded that the entire town was in attendance. Tippi and Ophie, Deputy Toolin, Reverend Arkley and his wife, and so many others she'd come to know and befriend since moving to Hollow Creek. An older couple, whom she'd heard introduced as Emilie's parents, arrived just minutes ago on the train from New York.

"McKenna! We're so glad you could make it." Tippi and Ophie both wrapped an arm around her.

"I'm so grateful your father allowed you to attend."

"He's still not happy with the calamity Tippi caused."

"Calamity?" Tippi frowned at her sister.

"Sorry. The *catastrophe*."

"It was not a catastrophe, and he never would have known about it—"

"Except for the dirty undercarriage of the Buick. That may have given him hints a plenty."

Tippi elbowed her sister. "No, it wasn't the dirty undercarriage. Some busybodies in Hollow Creek—fourteen of them, no less—saw fit to inform Father that they saw his motorcar in a ravine just outside of town."

"Fourteen busybodies? Goodness, but that's half the town."

Tippi and Ophie both laughed at McKenna's statement. "Well, at least all is forgiven. I could have been sent to live with our disagreeable and churlish aunt and uncle in Topeka." Tippi shivered for effect. "That would have been loathsome. I did have to pay for repairs out of my own savings, promise not to drive the Buick for an entire year, and pull weeds in the garden, but, yes, it could have been so much worse."

They visited further, catching up on happenings since they'd last seen each other. And McKenna realized that odd as it was, this town was more like home to her than Missoula.

Two of the maids distributed hors d'oeuvres and glasses of lemonade, and a table in the far corner boasted an abundant pile of presents, including the miniature wrapped purse McKenna brought.

Thad Evanson stood at the front of the parlor where furniture had been rearranged to accommodate the guests. Emilie and their children accompanied him, including a baby in Emilie's arms and a tiny girl in a wheelchair. "Thank you all for coming," said Thad. "And for joining us as we celebrate the newest member of the Evanson family." He lowered his tall self beside the wheelchair-bound girl. "This is Mamie Evanson. I hope you'll all give her a warm welcome."

The crowd clapped, and Thad waited until the applause ended before he continued. "We want to first and foremost thank the Lord for blessing us so richly with Adelia, Ephraim, Thad, Jr., and now Mamie. We also would like to thank the orphanage, our attorney who filed the paperwork for Mamie's adoption so quickly, and all of you. To have our family and friends share in this momentous occasion with us means everything.

"Please do make yourselves at home. There will be games and other festivities in the garden later this afternoon." He put an arm around Emilie.

She smiled up at him, then scanned the crowd. "I'm beginning to think we may need to hire a nanny to assist us with our passel full of children."

Everyone laughed at her comment, and McKenna immediately thought of Arrosa. If only she weren't ill, perhaps she could be a nanny for the Evansons. She loved children, and it would be a job she could do that didn't require intense scrubbing and cleaning as Mother's job did.

CHAPTER TWENTY-TWO

THE WEEKS PASSED QUICKLY, and McKenna and Clayton spent more time together—and in that time, she'd come to grow fonder of him. Fond of the witty stories he'd tell from his growing-up years—stories so different from her as a child. Fond of his dapper appearance and insistence on keeping the townsfolk of Hollow Creek safe. And fond of his extensive knowledge of the Bible. Someday she hoped to know as much about God's Word as he did.

She finished helping a customer, then relished the few moments of quiet to open the letter from Mother.

Dearest McKenna,

I hope this finds you doing well. For the first time since we moved to Thorburn Flats, Arrosa was able to sit outside on the porch three days ago. While it was only for a half hour, the sunshine did her well. She says to tell you hello and that she is hoping the pain in her wrists and hands will allow her to write to you soon. The doctor visited yesterday. Arrosa is still so weak, but the doctor assures us that in time, she will regain more of her strength. He did mention that there is a chance she could have heart issues and continued pain in her joints. Such news was difficult for Arrosa to hear, and I fear she has slipped into a melancholy thinking of what her future may hold.

Would you please pray for Arrosa? Pastor Shay preached a timely sermon last Sunday about the effectiveness of prayer. I have been learning how to pray and am endeavoring to do it with regularity.

Father's trial has been rescheduled to October. Please tell your sheriff friend thank you for all his aid in securing an attorney for your father. This man is far better than the last and was able to convince the judge to allow Father to stay in Bleakney until his trial.

I am happy to hear that the sheriff is not as vexing as you once thought. Perhaps someday when Arrosa is able to travel, we can pay a visit to Hollow Creek to meet him.

Thank you for all of your hard work at the boutique. I love you, miss you, and can't wait for my family to be together again.

All my love,
Mother

As they always did after McKenna read a letter from Mother, her eyes misted. Oh, but to be near her family again! To have Arrosa well and Father released from jail.

Father.

What a blessing he would be able to stay in Bleakney while awaiting trial. She was so grateful Clayton had convinced his uncle to represent Father. She offered a prayer of gratitude for the Lord's Providence in keeping her father in the small-town jail rather than him being transported to Missoula or even Deer Lodge.

Despite being in a better jail, she knew Father was lonely. He loved being around people and had always been a chattering sort about business matters with his colleagues. Colleagues that no longer acknowledged him after his crime. Was he hungry as well? He'd lost so much weight the last time she'd seen him.

Perhaps...

An idea percolated in her mind. What if she were to make Father's favorite cookies and ask Clayton if he could deliver them on his way to the sheriffs' meeting in two days? Such would for certain encourage Father.

She locked the store, hurried to the back of the building, and up the stairs to the apartment. She'd see what ingredients she needed and hopefully, the mercantile would allow her to charge any necessities. If not, perhaps she could find something to sell as it would be some time before McKenna earned further wages.

The few possessions she owned were tucked in a trunk, and McKenna rummaged through her meager clothing options, stationery, two hair ribbons, and one pair of shoes, in addition to the new pair she wore. She bit her lip. There had to be something to sell.

She rifled through the items again. Only when something clunked to the bottom of the trunk did she find a piece of jewelry she'd long forgotten.

McKenna held the aquamarine glass brooch between her forefinger and thumb and peered through the lovely transparent glass. Why did she still have this? How had it managed to not be commandeered with the rest of the family jewelry? How had it escaped her attention?

Whatever the reason, her heart soared at discovering it. If the mercantile decided to purchase it, or better yet, she could sell it at the boutique, she could use that money for both her idea and to send some extra to Mother and Arrosa.

McKenna tapped her chin. She could attempt to sell it in the shop, but it was doubtful it would sell in one day and she needed the funds posthaste so she could send the goodies with Clayton. After all, the brooch meant nothing to her. Leonard had given it to her once upon a time when they were courting. Back then, she supposed it sealed the growing feelings between them. But in hindsight, her feelings for Leonard were nothing more than friendship.

An hour later, she'd sold the brooch, finished her day at the boutique, confirmed with Clayton that he'd be happy to deliver the cookies if the jail allowed it, and was back at the apartment whipping up the batter for the cookies. McKenna added the sugar, one egg, softened butter, rolled oats, salt, and vanilla, scooped them onto a teaspoon, plopped them on the inverted pan she'd found in the apartment when she'd moved in, and shaped them much as she would were she making a macaroon.

She inhaled the delicious aroma of the Scottish Fancies, Father's favorite cookie. His mother, McKenna's grandmother, had arrived from Scotland and brought this and many other recipes with her. Sadly, McKenna had never met any of her grandparents before they passed. Cook baked these cookies often—so often in fact—that McKenna had the recipe memorized from the many times Cook allowed her and Arrosa to assist.

Next, she scrounged around for a tin in which to place the cookies. She located an old cocoa tin in a pot on the top shelf where she'd not yet perused. McKenna placed a dozen cookies inside, leaving five out, one for her, and four for Clayton.

Wouldn't Father be ecstatic when he received his Scottish Fancies!

Ma's urging hadn't made things any easier. Clayton did *not* want to meet with Hal. While he'd known the man a large portion of his life, it didn't mean he wanted him to marry Ma.

He dismounted, tethered his horse, and strode to Hal's front door. Would Hal really expect Ma to move from the home she'd shared with Pa and Clayton and live in Hal's house after they married? What of her mementos from Pa? It just didn't seem right.

"Hello, son. I was expecting you." Hal opened the door and waved Clayton inside.

Men called younger men "son" all the time. But something about Hal calling him that set Clayton's nerves on edge.

"Care for some lemonade?" Hal chuckled. "No, don't worry. I didn't make it myself. Your ma made it and sent me home with a pitcher. I'm surprised it's lasted this long."

"In that case, I'll take some."

Clayton attempted to keep the bite out of his tone. Hadn't he prayed just this morning for the Good Lord to guide his words? To temper his tongue?

Hal poured them each a cup and waved Clayton back out to the porch. "Might as well sit outside since it's a mite bit cooler today."

Clayton didn't care where they sat. He just wanted the meeting done and over with.

"Weather sure is nice this time of year. Sure am thankful we've had sufficient rain."

"Yes, I'm thankful we aren't having a drought this year."

They sat for a few minutes in awkward silence. Finally, Hal spoke. "You still living above the barbershop?"

"Yes, sir." This could be a lengthy meeting if they only discussed pleasantries. Of course, pleasantries made avoiding the topic they needed to discuss easier.

All right by Clayton.

"So I reckon your ma has told you that I aim to ask her to be my wife."

He had to give it to Hal. The man didn't mince words. "Yes, sir."

"How do you feel about that?"

Men didn't talk about their feelings, and Clayton wasn't about to start now. He shrugged.

"I recall when I lost my pa as a young'un." Hal stared off into the distance. "It was hard. My ma had the four of us, and there were times we had nothing to eat."

"Sorry to hear that." And he was.

"I was the oldest, so of course, it was up to me to work hard and support the family, even if I was only eight when Pa passed." Hal's voice broke a bit. "I would have done anything for Ma and my siblings. So I commenced taking care of things around the ranch. I was doing a fine job, even got out of school much of the time, which was fine with me." He chuckled again. "No one ever accused me of being one to cotton to school."

Clayton rocked the rocking chair and peered out over the acres dotted with cattle. While Hal's cabin was a humble one, he'd done well enough for himself with his sizable herd. He paid his bills on time at the mercantile and livery in Cullman. Clayton should know because he checked.

Hal exhaled a shaky breath. "All was well until Dwight came into our lives."

"Who was Dwight?"

"He was the man who thought he should marry Ma and raise us kids as his own."

"Was he a good man?"

"Oh, he was. Ma and Pa both knew him from when they went to school together as young'uns. She hadn't seen him in years until he stopped in town for a visit. He wasn't expecting Pa to have passed." Hal took a drink of his lemonade. "When he found out, he decided to help us on the ranch. I'd have none of it. Why should I allow this man I'd never met to be a hired hand when Ma had me?"

Clayton thought of all the questions he'd ask a man who'd just arrived in town. "Did he have a ranch of his own?"

"He did. Over near Butte. Also had worked in the copper mines. The man wasn't destitute by any stretch, and he knew how to work hard. 'Course, that may have been so he could persuade my ma he was worthy of her."

"How soon was this after your pa died?"

"Two years or so. Since Ma had known him years before, she and Dwight seemed to pick up where they left off. Meanwhile, I was fit to be tied as the saying goes. Even more so when he proposed to Ma six months later." Hal shook his head. "Did all I could to hate that man. But none of it worked."

A stab of his conscience niggled Clayton right in the gut. He didn't want to like Hal, but truth of the matter was, he always had liked and respected the man. "Didn't work, huh?"

"Nope. Not one bit. Dwight treated my ma like the lady she was, cared for us as though we were his own, sold his place in Butte so he could live in our house, which I appreciated because I didn't want to move to Butte." Hal set his cup on the round wooden table between them. "My sisters and brother took to him right away. Then he and Ma had two more children. All the while, I acted like he was my worst enemy."

"Did you ever accept him?"

"Yep. When I was fourteen and he saved my ma's life when she was sick with the influenza. As if he hadn't done enough for our family, he did that too. It was as though the flickering candlelight in my mind finally became brighter. That or maybe God got a hold of me. He knew I needed a good kick in the backside for the way I'd treated Dwight those years prior."

Clayton drained the remaining lemonade. "I'm glad it all worked out for you."

"Me too. I never forgot Pa and how much I loved him, but truth was, the Lord blessed me with two fathers." Hal rubbed his bearded chin. "What I'm trying to say in my roundabout way is that I love your ma. Have for a while. I want only what's best for her, and truth of the matter is I'd give my life for her." Hal's voice wavered. "But I know you ain't fond of the fact I love her."

"No, sir, I'm not." There. He'd said it.

"Can't blame you one bit. Like I said, I felt the same way about Dwight."

"I loved my pa." The lump in his throat made it difficult to swallow.

"I know you did. I thought of him as a good friend, like a brother to be exact. Your ma loved him something fierce, and he loved her. I have no right to try to diminish the love they felt for each other, nor would I. But I do love her, and if she'll have me, I'd consider myself the luckiest man alive."

Clayton gripped the handles of the rocking chair and kept his gaze on the fields. Why couldn't things like this be easier? "I like you, Hal. I know you're a good man, I just don't want to see Pa replaced."

"Your pa can never be replaced. Ever. I don't aim to replace him in your ma's life or yours. Although I do have to say that I'd be right honored to have you as a son. If you were my boy, I'd be prouder of you than any man could be proud of any son. And I mean that, sure as the day is long."

Hal's words, which Clayton knew were sincere, evoked an emotion in him he couldn't discern.

"I know, I know, this isn't easy. Believe me, I have spent time with the Lord over it, talked with your ma about it, and sought godly counsel. I don't want to do anything to sever the relationship you have with your mother, nor do I want to make an enemy of you. Rather, I'd like your blessing."

"My blessing?"

"Yes, son, I would. If you feel comfortable giving it. I promise to love your ma all the rest of the days the Lord gives me here on earth. I'll care for her and make sure she wants for nothing, well except maybe one of those newfangled automobiles. Can't see myself buying one of those anytime soon."

His words brought a smile to Clayton's lips. "I wouldn't mind having one."

"Well, you young folks can have them. Me, I'm a horse and wagon man. But if your ma wants one, I'll save up and buy her one."

"She doesn't. She's a horse and wagon woman."

Hal laughed. "Good to know."

The only sound for the next several minutes was the thumping of the rocking chairs rocking on the porch, cows mooing in the distance, and a bumblebee buzzing nearby. Would it be so wrong to give Hal his blessing? To gain a second father? More importantly, to see his mother happy? What if he was in love and wanted to marry a girl but couldn't secure the permission of her family member? McKenna's face flashed unannounced in his mind.

He released the breath he'd been holding and turned to face Hal. "All right, sir, you have my blessing."

"You mean it?"

"Yes."

Hal jumped up and did a little jig right there on the porch. "Looks like I'm gonna be a married man after all. Thank you, son. You won't regret it." He extended a hand to Clayton.

And deep down inside, Clayton knew he'd made the right choice.

Chapter Twenty-Three

CLAYTON DIDN'T MIND TRAVELING by rail. It gave him about a half hour of shut-eye before they reached Bleakney. He'd have just enough time to meet with Mr. Chapman before the train continued to Missoula for the sheriffs' meeting.

He held the tin in his hands, remembering how delicious the Scottish Fancies tasted. He could have easily eaten an entire tin were it not promised to someone else. He thought of McKenna and how he planned to ask her father about courting her. Would he be amenable? Would he speak to Clayton at all seeing as how he was a lawman? Surely having been arrested had left a sour taste. And if he did agree to meet with him, would he find Clayton suitable to court his daughter?

As if in response to his musings, Clayton brushed off his jeans and dusted off his cowboy hat. He made decent wages as a lawman, but couldn't ever give McKenna the life she'd previously had. He sometimes worked long hours, and a lawman was never off duty, so there would be times she would be alone. He was saving money to buy a home, but for now, she'd have to live above the barbershop. Would she be amenable to that?

Suddenly, a case of nerves overtook him. Perhaps he ought to ask for a raise and buy a home first before he sought to court McKenna. But then, courtship didn't always lead to marriage. In this case, he hoped it would.

Besotted jobbernowl.

Clayton was unable to catch any shut-eye due to rehearsing in his mind several times how he would ask Mr. Chapman if he could court McKenna. After the man ate the cookies, because, as Ma always said, *"Never ask a man anything important unless his belly is full."* Eating a dozen cookies—yes, Clayton had counted them—would stave off any man's hunger.

On schedule, the train pulled into the Bleakney Depot. Clayton strode to the jail, cookie tin in hand.

"Gern, great to see you," said Clayton when he entered the dismal jail.

"Beringer. Haven't seen you in a coon's age." The deputy clapped him on the shoulder. "What brings you to our fine hotel?"

Clayton laughed at Gern's description of the sheriff's office and jail. "I'm here to see one of your inmates."

"Oh?"

"Man by the name of Chapman."

"Yep. He's here." Gern squinted. "Just curious. What business do you have with Chapman?" His eyes veered to the cookie tin.

"I need to speak with him and pass these along from his daughter in Hollow Creek. Would that be all right?"

Gern shrugged. "Sure. How about I have him meet you in the extra room toward the back?"

"Are you afraid he'll escape?"

"He won't run. He's one of the nicest prisoners I've ever met. Just made some mistakes is all." Gern led him down the narrow hall past a few other outlaws to the far end. "Got a visitor here to see you, Chapman." Gern unlocked the jail cell.

"Mr. Chapman, my name is Sheriff Clayton Beringer from Hollow Creek."

The older man shrank back slightly before recovering. "Is something amiss?"

"No, sir. Just would like to speak with you a minute or two."

Gern opened the cell door. "You can meet in the extra room. I'll put you back in when you're finished," he said to Chapman.

In the extra room, which boasted a table, two chairs, and wanted posters on the otherwise empty walls, Chapman took a seat across from Clayton.

"I'll be back in a few minutes to check on things," said Gern, closing and locking the door behind them.

Chapman was a thin fellow with brown hair and graying temples, hazel eyes, ungroomed whiskers peppered with gray, and a weary countenance. "I've been a model prisoner," Chapman offered, setting his hands on the table, removing them, then resting them again on the table.

Clayton regarded him, attempting to reconcile in his mind that this was the father of the woman he'd come to love. "Sir, I'm not here to chastise your time as an inmate. I'm here to give you these." He set the tin on the table. "These are from McKenna."

"McKenna?"

"Yes, sir. I am traveling from Hollow Creek, where I'm a lawman, to Missoula for a meeting, and she asked me to stop by here and deliver these. Said they were your favorite kind. I admit I ate the four she gave me in one bite." He smiled, hoping to help alleviate some of Chapman's obvious distress.

The man opened the tin. "Scottish Fancies. My favorite." With a shaky hand, he scooped one out of the tin and took a bite. He closed his eyes as he did so, chewing the cookie slowly. "My mother made these for us often. Then Cook did as well." He faltered on the last words. "But none of those cookies tasted as delicious as these." Chapman took another bite, then reached for a second. "Would you care for one?"

"No, sir." There was no way Clayton would prevent the man from enjoying his present to the fullest, even if Clayton's own stomach rumbled at the sight of the treats.

"You know McKenna, then?"

"I do." He'd wait a bit before asking Chapman the question that had been on his mind for some time now.

"How is she?"

"She's doing fine. Working hard at the boutique."

Chapman smiled and moistened his chapped lips. "That's excellent news. She always was fond of the latest fashions. I appreciated Julia Mathilda giving her the opportunity."

Clayton had his own opinions of Miss Mathilda, but he didn't say as much.

The man finished another cookie, then replaced the lid. "Please forgive me for my gluttony. I find it impossible to stop eating Scottish Fancies once I start. They remind me of better days." He cleared his throat. "Finding myself in jail was not something I ever anticipated. I was a highly respected banker in one of Missoula's most reputable banks."

Clayton nodded, not knowing what to say in response. Most of the outlaws he apprehended and locked up would say they never anticipated finding themselves in jail.

"One minute we were living with abundant wealth. The next..." He peered down at his folded hands. Hands folded so tightly his knuckles had turned white. Dark circles beneath his eyes proved he hadn't slept much. "We purchased an additional home, traveled extensively, and lived beyond our means. I bought three automobiles. When Arrosa—our other daughter—became ill, I spent ghastly amounts of money for 'cures' that never worked. Soon, our debt exceeded our income. Yet, we continued to spend. Not sure why I'm telling you all of this, I guess I just need you to know that it was never supposed to end this way."

"I'm sorry about your younger daughter. McKenna mentioned how sick she is."

"It's hard for a man to watch his child succumb to an illness. It's his job to provide for and protect his family. When the debt rose so much I couldn't fulfill the payment obligations, I felt I had no choice. It was wrong, and I claim full responsibility." He sighed. "I don't expect you to understand."

Clayton had heard many excuses in his time as a sheriff. Excuses he didn't believe, didn't agree with, and didn't give heed to. But looking at the man in front of him, sincerity in his eyes and remorse in his countenance, Clayton knew what he spoke was not just a meaningless excuse. It was regret that he'd likely do anything to fix. "I appreciate you sharing that with me."

"Just want you to know I'm not like the usual criminal. I plan to pay back every penny and my debt to society, and someday, Lord willing, I will be free again. I've sought His forgiveness, but it will be some time before I forgive myself for my poor choices."

Hopefully, Clayton's Uncle Art would be able to convince the court to work a deal with Chapman. The man was earnest in his regret, unlike many of the criminals Clayton had dealt with. "Sometimes it's hardest to forgive ourselves. But the way I see it is that if the Lord, being Holy and blameless—the Creator of all things—the One who sent His Son to die for our sins—can forgive us, surely we can, with His help, forgive ourselves."

"You make an excellent point. I've only just recently started my journey toward knowing the Lord and surrendering my life to Him."

They continued talking for the next several minutes until Clayton finally developed the courage to ask his question. "I was wondering if I could have your permission to court your daughter."

Chapman's eyebrows lifted to his forehead, and Clayton's words spilled quicker than he'd planned. "I can provide for her, sir. I have a good job as a lawman, I have an apartment above the barbershop but am saving to purchase a house, and I'll love and care for her all the days of my life."

"Does she feel the same for you?"

Did she feel the same for him as he felt for her? Would she say yes if he asked for her hand in courtship? He involuntarily shrugged. "I—hope so?" Not meant to be a question, but exited his mouth as one anyway.

"I don't know you well enough to..."

"Deputy Gern here can vouch for me, as can any of the lawmen in Hollow Creek, Cullman, and Missoula Counties."

They spoke for the next few minutes before Gern entered the room. Upon his recommendation, Chapman gave Clayton permission to court McKenna.

McKenna liked Clayton's mother from the first time she met her. The kindly woman with the same hazel eyes as Clayton and a contagious laugh readily accepted McKenna. So unlike the former *friends* she'd had in Missoula. Friends who appreciated her friendship only until the Chapman family became an "embarrassment."

Clayton's job demanded he finish a few items before the three of them met at Olga's Café for the noonday meal. In the meantime, Mrs. Beringer asked to see the boutique.

Something akin to pride filled McKenna as she opened the door of the shop and ushered in Mrs. Beringer.

"Oh, what a lovely store!" The older woman flitted through, commenting on several of the garments before reaching the shelf with the jewelry and handbags. She picked one of the three cameo brooches from the collection. "This is beautiful. It reminds me of one my ma had when I was a child. My pa had given it to her for their wedding anniversary."

McKenna would tuck that piece of information into her mind for later.

Clayton entered the boutique. "Never thought I'd visit here as much as I do," he said with a chuckle.

"And not for just chasing and apprehending criminals," added McKenna.

One of Mrs. Beringer's eyebrows crept into her hairline. "Something tells me there's a story here."

Clayton grinned at her, and McKenna's heartbeat quickened and turned over in response. He held her gaze. Could he see the affection in her eyes? That she cared for him deeply? She dipped her head, still maintaining the special moment between them.

Several seconds ticked by before she remembered Mrs. Beringer was in the building. "But goodness. I suppose we should make arrangements to go to the mercantile."

"The mercantile?" Clayton asked.

"Yes. Not the mercantile." McKenna recovered slower than she'd wanted to from her flustered error. "Yes, Olga's," she repeated to no one in particular.

A grin jotted across Mrs. Beringer's face.

Did the woman suspect that McKenna was falling in love with her son?

Clayton hadn't considered marriage a whole lot. After all, he had other things on his mind like justice and protecting the town he'd come to love. Hopefully securing the confidence of the townsfolk for the next election. Doing his best to ignore Rantz and staying alive when he tracked down criminals. Those things permeated his thoughts and left little room for women, courtship, and other romantic notions.

And he *was* a man. Men didn't think about those things.

Well, not until McKenna Chapman had come into his life. Now she was pretty much all he thought about. Wiley would tell him he was flutterpated, some relatively new word Wiley had stumbled across in some dictionary. Of course, Wiley was one to talk. It was clear as the nose on his face that he was in love with Tippi Harkins. That realization would leave Wiley little time to read books, especially the dictionary.

The pleasing rosy pink dotting McKenna's face made it impossible for him to stifle a grin. She was beautiful. Her appearance, her personality, and the way she cared for others. He appreciated her wit and charm and her excitement for her newfound faith in the Lord.

So, yes, Clayton Beringer was considering marriage. On a daily basis.

But lest Ma think he was flutterpated, he best return his thoughts to more *important* matters at hand. Like the noonday meal. He offered an elbow to both Ma and McKenna, and together they strolled to the café after McKenna locked the shop.

It made him happy that the two most important women in his life shared a good camaraderie. He opened the door of the café, and they took their seats in the far corner where he and McKenna most often sat when they patronized the business.

"Did you ever catch that Salazar fellow?" Ma asked after they'd ordered their lunch.

"We did." His attention lingered on McKenna. What if things had turned out differently? How many times had he rehashed the scenario in his mind that she may very well have been injured or worse were it not for God's hand in the matter?

"I hope it wasn't too terribly dangerous." This time, Ma's penetrating stare reminded him that her concern for him was intensified due to having lost Pa while he was working to ensure justice. If she knew some of the perilous obstacles he faced, she'd fret and then fret some more.

"Not as dangerous as it could have been." There. Not a lie, as he prided himself on being honest, but just a slight skirting of the issue.

Thankfully, that seemed to satisfy her. "Last time we spoke, you mentioned he had stolen jewelry from McKenna's shop and also two horses. Were they recovered?"

"The horses were. Thankfully we found them in time before they were malnourished, killed, or sold to someone else. We never would have recovered them then. As for the jewelry, only two pieces were found. Salazar efficiently sold the rest."

Ma gripped his hand. "I'm so proud of you, son. Your pa would have been so proud of you too."

"Thank you, but it wasn't all my doing. McKenna helped as did the sheriffs from Cullman and Missoula."

"Be that as it may, you're doing a fine job upholding the law."

He appreciated Ma's encouragement. Were it not for her steadfast belief he could do this job, he'd never have succeeded.

When his mother left for a moment to speak with one of the townsfolk she knew, McKenna inclined toward him. "She found a cameo brooch in the boutique today. Perhaps we could mention it to Hal for a wedding gift."

Clayton had heard of the brooch his grandfather had given his grandmother for their anniversary. Sadly, it was lost and never recovered. If he had the funds himself, he'd purchase it for Ma. He pondered McKenna's suggestion. To receive it from her new husband would mean a lot to his mother. "I'll mention it to him." A few weeks ago, he would have done anything to keep Hal from endearing himself more to Ma. But things had changed after his conversation with the man—and the Lord's subsequent softening of Clayton's heart toward Hal.

After the noonday meal, he rode with Ma back to Cullman. Tomorrow after church, he and McKenna would go for their weekly drive. And he hoped to muster more courage than it took to apprehend the vilest of criminals to ask her the question on his mind.

Chapter Twenty-Four

"WE WISH TO THANK everyone again for all of their assistance in rebuilding the Hoekstra family's home," said Reverend Arkley during the announcements at church the following day. "While there was a delay in receiving the lumber from the mill and the shingles for the roof, the house is now completed. Mr. Hoekstra would like to address the congregation."

Joy built in McKenna's heart. She had been there that day to help the women with the meals. When she lived in Missoula, Mother often arranged charity functions, which McKenna and Arrosa happily attended. However, if McKenna was honest, it was mainly for appearance's sake rather than to bless someone in need.

The same couldn't be said, however, for her role in aiding the Hoekstras. The family was poor, and after having lost all of their belongings, owned even less. But the town had come together to ensure they wouldn't be homeless.

An endeavor of which McKenna had been a part because she cared. Not for appearance's sake. Not to receive something in return. But to show the love of Christ. She blinked back the tears as Mr. Hoekstra told of how, without God's Providence and the congregation's help, they would not have had a home for the upcoming cold winter months.

Clayton squeezed her hand, his calloused one wrapping around her much smaller one with ease. Her heart leaped in her chest at his comforting touch. Loving him meant not only spending time with him and enjoying his company, but perhaps even more opportunities to serve. When Reverend Arkley spoke of God changing people's hearts, McKenna never imagined He could change her heart. But He had in more ways than one.

After the services, Clayton assisted her into the buggy he'd rented from the livery. "One of these days, I'm going to rent us an automobile."

"As long as you're a better driver than Tippi."

He laughed and winked at her, causing butterflies to take up residency in McKenna's stomach.

"Can't say I won't be tempted to speed around the corners a time or two, but I aim to keep it on the road and out of the ravine."

It was her turn to laugh. "Poor Tippi. Her father still has not allowed her to drive the horseless carriage. I feel sympathy for Ophie as well. Her chances of borrowing the motorcar are slim thanks to her sister's accidental adventure. But truly, as delightful as a drive in an automobile would be, I don't mind the buggy."

Clayton sobered. "You know I'll never be an affluent man."

"And I'll never again be an affluent woman."

"I just wanted you to know that I wouldn't be able to offer you the things that you were accustomed to in Missoula."

If only Clayton knew just how much that didn't matter to her. That things were just that...items that could be taken away or lost at a moment's notice. It hadn't been an easy road for McKenna since she still at times longed for beautiful garments and sparkling jewelry and probably always would, but Jesus had placed in her heart the yearning for much more important things.

A jolt rocked the buggy, and Wiley tilted his head inside. "Are you two lovebirds going to sit here all day or are you going to put the money you paid to rent the buggy to good use and go for a drive?"

"You're a dolt, Wiley. Reckon we won't just sit here all day."

"Could have fooled me." He stood up straighter, but his attempt to add any further height to his scrawny stature failed. "Meanwhile, I'd love to stay and prattle on about buggies and such, but I am meeting Tippi at her house for the noonday meal." He lowered his voice. "I think she's grown quite fond of me."

"No one said she was the wisest of women."

Wiley slugged Clayton in the arm, then pulled back his wrist, shook it, and pretended to wince. "Teach me not to punch my best friend." But as quickly as he offered his theatrics, he sobered. "Guess I best be on my way. Good day to you both." He tipped his fedora then strutted to his horse.

"I give them until next summer to marry," said Clayton.

"Or before. Tippi mentioned offhandedly that she's always wanted a Christmas wedding."

Clayton chuckled and flicked the reins, and McKenna settled into the soft leather seat. Today they would once again go to their favorite place, a piece of land near a babbling creek just outside of town. Perhaps someday when Father was released from jail, her family might consider moving to Hollow Creek. She offered another prayer for them and thanked the Lord once again that Clayton's uncle was willing to represent Father and had already made great headway in a case the former attorney had all but forgotten and neglected.

They bumped along the uneven ground to the clearing by the creek. Clayton had built a bench from logs and hauled it here the last time they visited. His hands lingered on her waist when he assisted her from the buggy, and for a moment she thought he might kiss her.

Oh, they'd already shared a kiss since Father gave his blessing for courtship. She stared into the eyes of the man who'd won her heart.

"May I steal a kiss?" The flirtatious glimmer in his hazel eyes convinced her more than his words had.

"Yes, you may." McKenna's heart hammered against her chest, and she feared were it not for his strong arms around her, her legs would buckle beneath her. His mouth claimed hers in a series of three kisses before he drew gently away.

"Reckon I should get our lunch from the buggy."

"Indeed." But her word came out as more of a breathless gasp.

He retrieved the basket of food she'd packed before church and set it on the ground beside the bench. They prayed, then ate their sandwiches. "I heard this property is for sale," Clayton said between bites.

"Really?"

"I've considered purchasing it."

His declaration caught her unawares. "It is a lovely piece of property."

"It is. Just a short distance from the sheriff's office and with the best view in the county." He pointed to a clearing not far from where they sat. "I'd build a house right there."

The scent of wildflowers blew their way, and McKenna inhaled. "I could never grow tired of sitting here by the creek. I've been to a lot of places in my life, including other countries, but I've never seen a more perfect setting."

"We could sit on the porch in a pair of rocking chairs on warm summer days. In the winter, we'd have the view of the snow-capped mountains."

Had he meant to say *we*?

McKenna glanced at him, and a broad smile crossed his face. "What do you think about that?" he asked.

"About the rocking chairs and snow-capped mountains?" Her thoughts were a jumbled mess, and her voice came out as more of a squeak. Dare she believe their future held the prospect of marriage? Of course, many courtships did, hers and Leonard's notwithstanding.

"Sure. About that and about living in a house on this property. It wouldn't be a big house. More like a cabin, but it would be..."

Clayton slid off the bench and dropped to his knees. He took her hand in his and rubbed the back of it tenderly with his calloused thumb.

Did women routinely faint when the prospect of marriage loomed? She held her breath, and her heart danced. Would he say the words she thought he might say?

"McKenna, I love you. I know I can't offer you the largest and fanciest home or the finest clothes. You'll likely be riding around in a wagon or on horseback for years before I can afford an automobile. While I haven't yet asked your pa for his blessing—but I do plan to—I promise you that if you'll have me, I'll love you and care about you forever."

"Yes."

"Yes, you'll marry me?"

"Yes, I'll marry you."

He grabbed her other hand and pulled her from the bench and into his arms. "A kiss to celebrate?" he asked, a twinkle in those handsome hazel eyes she'd grown to love.

McKenna nodded as his lips met hers.

Epilogue
The Following Spring

THE MONTANA SPRING AIR carried on it the scent of promise. Clayton lifted McKenna from the buggy, and together they stood, hand-in-hand in front of their new home.

McKenna released a contented sigh. God was so good. While things looked bleak for a time, He was faithful. Oh, so faithful.

Father had given his blessing for Clayton to marry McKenna soon after Clayton's proposal. He would serve another year in the Bleakney jail, then would be released with the order to repay the remaining money owed to the bank. Clayton's Uncle Art had been instrumental in Father being able to remain there rather than be transferred to Deer Lodge. And he'd not charged Father a cent for his representation.

Not only that, but the judge agreed, under the supervision of Deputy Gern in Bleakney, that Father would be allowed to attend the wedding in Hollow Creek three months ago, then be promptly transported back to jail. Never had McKenna seen her father look so proud as when he walked her down the aisle of Grace Church.

Arrosa continued to improve and, while weak, had started to walk with a cane. Her wrists and ankles afforded her pain from time to time, but overall, the Lord had performed a miracle in healing her. Next month, she'd arrive in Hollow Creek to potentially work as a nanny for the Evansons. McKenna could scarcely wait.

Mother recently obtained a job at the Bellerose Hotel and Restaurant cleaning the hotel rooms until she could come to assist McKenna in Hollow Creek with working at the boutique. If all went well, McKenna's entire family would reside here after Father was released from jail.

Although, McKenna knew her time managing the boutique would soon come to an end. One couldn't very well operate a shop when she was busy caring for a husband and an infant. She placed a hand on her belly. Eight months from now, she and Clayton would be proud parents.

Tippi and Wiley were married three days before Christmas. Clayton's mother and Hal had married in February, and Hal presented Mrs. Beringer with the cameo brooch from the boutique, much to her delight.

Clayton reached over and tucked a hair behind her ear. "Well, Mrs. Beringer, shall we go inside our new home? Quite a stretch from our apartment above the barbershop these past months."

"Indeed."

He lifted her into his strong arms, planted a passionate kiss on her lips, and stepped up the porch stairs and through the front door of their new home.

McKenna couldn't help but smile at the joy budding up in her chest. Only God could orchestrate new beginnings from such painful circumstances. Never had she anticipated making her home in this small town. And never had she anticipated there would be love in store for her in Hollow Creek, Montana.

READ A SNEAK PEEK FROM

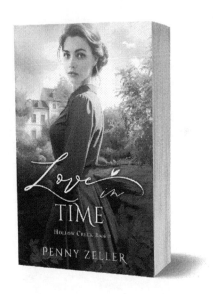

CAN LOVE HEAL TWO
WOUNDED HEARTS?

LOVE IN TIME

SNEAK PEEK

MISSOULA, MONTANA, 1913

Had she just heard him correctly? He wished to dine with her for the noonday meal at the Bellerose Restaurant?

Wayne Lingis was awaiting her answer, and she was sitting there in her dumbfounded state. Her gaze met his, and he smiled.

That dapper smile she'd been fond of all these years. Her heart pounded in her chest, and she felt the blush creep up the back of her neck and onto her face. Did Wayne notice?

Arrosa Chapman took a deep breath. How not to sound overly thrilled even though she was—that was the question. "Yes, Wayne. That sounds lovely."

"Perfect. I'll meet you at the Bellarose Restaurant in two hours. At least it's not far to walk."

Her smile was one of hesitance. It may not be far for him or even for her were it not for her current circumstances. But as such, she'd need to give herself plenty of time to traverse the gift shop, through the hotel's main foyer, and to the restaurant on the other side.

"I look forward to it. Good to see you again, Arrosa."

She watched him leave with his purchase, his confident swagger one she'd memorized from all those years ago when she was secretly fond of him during their school years and beyond.

How was she supposed to wait calmly for the next two hours? Especially if the number of customers was lacking? The time would undoubtedly crawl by. They had much to converse about, and she wanted to hear all about his time at dental school in Chicago.

A thought popped into her mind unannounced. What of Father's incarceration for embezzlement? Did Wayne know? If he didn't and he found out, would that affect his desire to partake in a noonday meal with her? To have anything to do with her at all? Arrosa worried her bottom lip. When their family fell upon hard times, Father made an unfortunate choice—a choice for which he ultimately was caught and the Chapmans lost everything. During that time, Arrosa became ill with rheumatic fever, and now, all this time later, Father remained in jail in Bleakney, a town not far from Missoula. And Mother and Arrosa, with her sister, McKenna's help, started over with nothing but a few clothes and a drafty and dilapidated apartment in a neglected and poverty-stricken part of town.

But God had been faithful. Oh, Mother would mention that day after day while Arrosa lay in bed with pain and fatigue so horrible she couldn't move. And it was true. While Arrosa had never given much thought to the Lord before all of this transpired, she was beginning to understand just *how* faithful He was. And who He was. And what He'd done for her.

Two customers entered, perused the tiny shop, then left. Arrosa peered at the clock on the shelf. An hour left. She'd be sure to start her journey to the restaurant beforehand because it took her a significant amount of time to hobble along, and she'd be exhausted when she reached the table. No sense in Wayne seeing her huffing and puffing to catch her breath.

What should she say if he asked about Father? Should she volunteer the information? The Lingis Family was affluent and would likely never allow their son to associate with the likes of her after Father's transgression. If only Wayne had taken interest in her years ago. After all, she'd fancied him and had admired him from afar. Well, mostly from afar. She could count on one hand the number of times they'd spoken more than a few words—the times he'd actually engaged in conversation with her.

Today was one of those times, and she wanted nothing to hinder their time together.

If you want to be among the first to hear about the next Hollow Creek installment, sign up for Penny's newsletter at www.pennyzeller.com. You will receive book and writing updates, encouragement, notification of current giveaways, occasional freebies, and special offers.

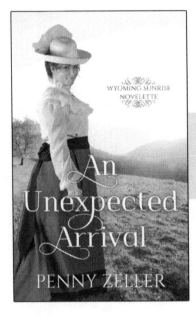

A
WYOMING
SUNRISE
NOVELETTE

If you enjoyed this glimpse into the lives of McKenna and Clayton, please consider leaving a review on your social media, Amazon, Goodreads, Barnes and Noble, or BookBub. Reviews are critical to authors, and those stars you give us are such an encouragement.

Author's Note

Dear Reader,

Thank you for taking a trip with me to Hollow Creek, Montana. For some of you, this may be your first trip, while for others, it's a return visit, having previously enjoyed *Love in Disguise*.

I was so grateful for the opportunity to write McKenna and Clayton's story. Within the first scenes of furiously typing, their characters came alive for me.

While fictional liberties are commonly taken in historical novels, such as Father being allowed to attend and participate in the wedding (it was unclear in my research whether they would allow a criminal awaiting trial to do this, although we see it oftentimes today), many things in the book were based on reality. For instance, the prices for the dentist and some of the merchandise prices were real. While Hollow Creek and Bleakney are fictitious towns, Missoula is real, as is the Deer Lodge prison. Our family visited the Old Montana Prison and Auto Museum in Deer Lodge, and it is a fascinating place. I would highly recommend a visit if you are in the area.

The poverty-stricken Thorburn Flats in Missoula was fictitious, although I am certain there were poorer areas in the city at that time. I took fictional liberties with the telephone exchange or lack thereof. However, retrieving the car from a ravine was inspired by a black and white photograph I saw of folks doing that very same thing with horses and several men at the helm attempting to remove the automobile. Speaking of automobiles, the 1910 Buick Surrey was a real automobile and a stunning one. Ackhurst Lady's Boots were fictional but McBride's Nerve and Bone Liniment was real.

Books aren't complete without a few bloopers. In this case, during the first round of editing, we discovered that Reverend Arkley "posted" something. Glad my editors caught that because in 1912, it was doubtful the reverend had a social media account. I also had typed that Clayton was hoping to envelope McKenna in the safety of his arms. Again, my wonderful editors caught that, and it was changed to have him envelop her in his arms.

During the writing of this book, my precious grandma, Nanie, passed. Having grown up in a neighboring house, our close-knit family would spend Christmas and Thanksgiving together each year for two decades. Not a day would pass when we didn't drive down our country dirt road past Nanie and Papa's house, and Nanie would be outside in her "Secret Garden" as she referred to it. We joked that we'd never seen anyone cram so many flowers, trees, and doodads into one small spot. Needless to say, she was an avid collector. She'd wave enthusiastically when we drove by or flag us down for a quick chat.

I dedicated *Love in Store* to my loving, spunky, and beautiful Swedish grandma because she was such an important part of my life and she was always supportive of my books from day one. I would send her handwritten and computer printouts of stories after we moved 650 miles away, and she'd faithfully read them and give me her input. She always told me I'd someday be a published author and encouraged me often over the years. When my first Christian historical romance released, she became my spokeswoman to those in my former hometown, including those in the Garden Society (for which Nanie served as president for numerous years). My grandma loved to read, especially historicals.

Nanie, together with Papa, who preceded her in death, took my sister, cousin, and me to church, always had a bowl of Rice Chex at the ready when we visited, and shared wonderful stories of her younger years and when her own parents emigrated to Ellis Island from Sweden as children. She loved to garden (which I inherited) and always talked about the "silly old people", of which she never was one. Not even in her 90s. Nanie is with Jesus now, and I know I'll see her again. But I sure miss her!

Arrosa's story is next on the agenda for the Hollow Creek Series and will be released next year. She's such a sweet and delicate soul, and I know you'll enjoy re-meeting her and the handsome ranch hand, Malachi Callahan, in *Love in Time*.

Another surprise? There are plans in the works for an Ophie Harkins Christmas novelette. Stay tuned.

Until we meet again, happy reading!

Blessings,

Penny

Acknowledgments

As always, I could not have written this book without the help of many. Thank you to my family, who continues to encourage, stand by me, and support me in this crazy writing life. (And it, indeed, is crazy at times!) A special thank you to my husband for his help with logistics in retrieving the Buick from the ravine and to my oldest for acting out the suspenseful scene with Pietro Salazar.

Thank you to my cousin, Josh Wageman, PhD, DPT, MPAS, who helped me with Arrosa's rheumatic fever diagnosis.

Thank you to my beta readers for being the first ones to read my books and offer invaluable suggestions.

Thank you to my Penny's Peeps, who are amazing in helping me spread the word about my books. You are always awesome, but especially this year when you've assisted me with several books in a short span of time.

Thank you to my launch team members who never hesitate in sharing about my book on their socials.

Thank you to my amazing developmental editor at Mountain Peak Edits & Design. Your awesome suggestions make my books the best they can be, and I appreciate you!

To my readers. May God bless and guide you as you grow in your walk with Him.

And, most importantly, thank you to my Lord and Savior, Jesus Christ. It is my deepest desire to glorify You with my writing and help bring others to a knowledge of Your saving grace.

ABOUT THE AUTHOR

Penny Zeller is known for her heartfelt stories of faith-filled happily ever afters and her passion to impact lives for Christ through fiction. Her books feature tender romance, steady doses of humor, and memorable characters that stay with you long after the last page. While she has had a love for writing since childhood, Penny began her adult writing career penning articles for national and regional publications on a wide variety of topics. Today Penny is a multi-published author of over two dozen books and is also a fitness instructor, loves the outdoors, and is a flower gardening addict.

In her spare time, she enjoys camping, hiking, kayaking, biking, bird watching, reading, running, and playing volleyball. Penny resides with her husband and two daughters in small-town America and loves to connect with her readers at her website at www.pennyzeller.com, her blog, www.pennyzeller.wordpress.com, and her Facebook page at www.facebook.com/pennyzellerbooks where she posts faith, funnies, writing updates, and encouragement. All of her socials can be found at https://linktr.ee/pennyzeller.

HOLLOW CREEK

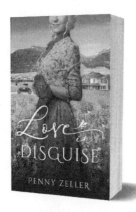

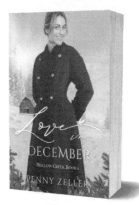

WYOMING SUNRISE

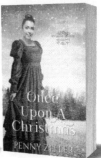

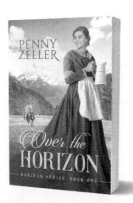

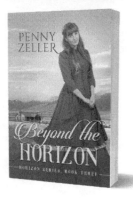

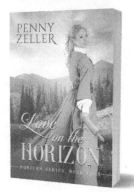

LOVE LETTERS FROM ELLIS CREEK

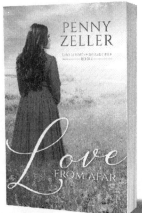

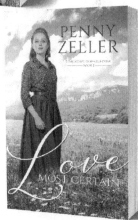

STANDALONE BOOKS

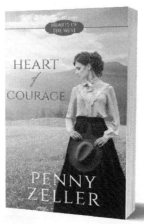

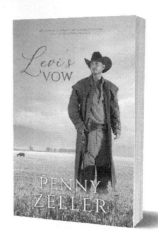

MOUNTAIN JUSTICE

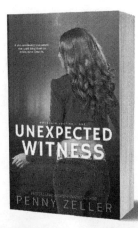

Who is he really?
And why is someone after him?

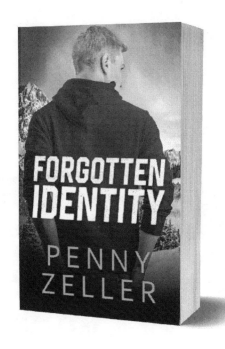

SMALL TOWN SHENANIGANS

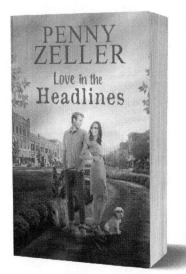

Chokecherry Heights

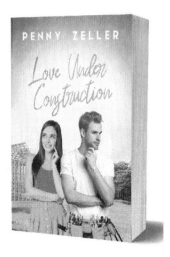